THE WAY IT ENDS

THE WAY IT ENDS

By

Theodore Jacobs

International Psychoanalytic Books (IPBooks)
New York • http://www.IPBooks.net

The Way It Ends
Published by IPBooks, Queens, NY
Online at: www.IPBooks.net

First paperback edition

ISBN 978-1-956864-43-4

For Jack, Jason and Dylan

Prologue

It's what he had dreaded. Word down from on high – an order.

Act now. Eliminate the threat or everything would be lost. Clearly it was a pointed reminder of his commitment, his pledge, and a warning. Disobedience would not be tolerated, would bring on the known consequences.

He understood, but they did not understand, did not appreciate his situation, the impossible place he was in. Nor, if they understood would they care. They recognized no personal ties. The enemy was the enemy and the enemy had to be eliminated.

He had avoided this as long as he could, but now it had arrived. Now there was no choice. He had to walk out the door and do what had to be done.

But he delayed, couldn't get himself to move. He sat for many more minutes. And when he did move, when he finally started for the place where the man was, where his target was, his gait was slow, his steps hesitant.

The boy had left and Lenny was alone on the narrow bed. He had been like this many times, alone in a room after the boy had gone. And it had been all right. He hadn't minded being so alone. But now it was different. The grayness had come back, grayness everywhere. It felt as though he'd been transported north, far north, to somewhere that was forever gray and misty, a land with little light, little sun. And the question that for months had plagued him, that had let up only while the boy was there, returned and pressed in on him insistently. Was this the time? The right time? With all that had happened, had not happened, could no longer happen, was this the time? He thought it was, had the deep feeling that it must be.

He rose, walked to the closet, opened the door. He was looking for something, a tool. He saw nothing, just his decrepit suitcase on the floor and trousers hanging on a rack. Nothing else. He knew well all that was in the room, but he looked around anyway. Alongside the bed was a night table and a lamp, its cord stretching behind the headboard to a socket by the floor. And a standing bookshelf containing a couple of books, a rickety-looking desk, and, in front of it, an uncomfortable straight-back chair. He sat in it, pulled it up to the desk, searched the drawers, and found a couple of sheets of notebook paper. He extracted them, set both sheets in front of him, and began to write. He'd been at it a short time, less than a half hour, when he heard knocking, light knocking. He did not respond, hoping whoever it was, the maid or whoever, would go away. He wanted to be alone. But the knocking continued louder now. He got himself up, concealed what he had written in one of the volumes on the bookshelf, and crossed to the door. He delayed a moment to compose himself. Then he opened it.

Chapter 1

In the more than two decades that I have been in psychiatric practice, I have heard many testimonies to premonitions, accounts of how, prior to some life-changing experience, a patient somehow "knew" that it was going to happen. I, myself, am not a believer. To me it is clear that these so-called premonitions are nothing more or less than tricks of the mind, unconscious deceptions that convert coincidence into a sense of fore knowledge, useful, for those who have a need to deny that life has caught them by surprise.

Nonetheless, when, for the first time in the twelve years that she had been with me, Linda, my secretary, broke an inviolate rule of mine and interrupted while I was in session with a patient, I had the instantaneous conviction that my life was about to be turned upside down.

My first thought was of what I dreaded most; something happening to my kids. Terrifying visions of Josh, my rebellious sixteen-year-old, lying dead on a highway after an auto accident; Emily, our darling eight-year-old, bleeding out in the ER, as she nearly did a year ago when an attack of ulcerative colitis— rare in young children—almost took away her life.

I, at the time, was working with a young woman suffering from agoraphobia when Linda rapped lightly on my door. I heard it, but it was so unexpected, so remote from where my mind was at the moment—absorbed in trying to find a thread in Mary's scattered communications—

that, for a moment I thought that the intensity of the work was getting to me and I was having an auditory hallucination.

When I realized that someone was at the door, I excused myself, crossed the room, and using my body as a shield to prevent whoever from looking in, opened it just enough to see out.

Linda whispered an apology, explained she thought I would want to know that two detectives were in the waiting room. Two detectives? I was startled. I felt my heart revving up. What in the world was this? My mind flashed to the thought that I was in trouble, that I had made a serious error of some kind; misdiagnosed a case with terrible consequences, failed to recognize that a patient who killed himself had actually been suicidal. My impulse was to break off the session, rush out, and find out what the hell they wanted, but I made myself hold back as my patient, Mary, was in distress. I could not leave her that way.

"Tell them I'm in session: I murmured. "I'll see them in ten minutes."

It was a bit longer before I got free. As the end of the session approached, Mary looked so anxious that I thought it best to sit with her a few extra minutes.

Then what I saw in the waiting room surprised me; the detectives I was familiar with, street operatives who, on occasion, dropped by to quiz me about a patient they had picked up for possession, were rough-hewn types, the sons of Irish or Italian immigrants who had come up through the ranks. They would appear in their work clothes; jeans, Nikes and sweatshirts, and address me as "Doc."

The two who sat side by side on my waiting room couch, an older, white man and a young Black woman, seemed a different order of detective. The man, large and heavy-set, was neatly dressed in a charcoal gray suit. The woman was light-skinned, slim, and lovely, an Audra MacDonald-type, someone you'd expect to find doing her Sondheim repertoire at the Carlyle.

They stood, the man, who must have weighed close to two-fifty, after having to make two tries to get up. They introduced themselves as Detective Martin and Detective Belker. We shook and I ushered them in. I took my usual place behind my desk and they sat on the two chairs that I used to accommodate the parents of the youngsters I worked with, as well as an occasional couple for marital therapy. The big Detective's bottom landed with such a crunching sound that I feared his chair would give way and not enhance my standing with the law.

Fortunately, this did not happen and he, who I judged to be in his mid-fifties, sat forward and addressed me in a way that caught me off guard.

"I am speaking with Dr. William Strickman, am I not?"

"You are." What the hell was this. I was used to the informality of the local guys.

"Hi ya, Doc," they'd say, "I'm Joe Smith from the 23rd. You got a minute?"

This man's approach was different in a way that aroused my curiosity and also made me anxious. I scanned his face. He was not smiling and he did not meet my eyes. He was looking past me, avoiding direct contact.

Seeing my puzzlement, he explained.

"We need to make sure that we're speaking to the right person, Doctor," he said. "Do you have a brother by the name of Leonard Strickman?"

"I do." Jesus, what in the world did this have to do with Lenny? Did he wander into the street and get hit by a truck? Given his way of losing himself in fantasy, that could happen. Or, in his absent-minded way, did he forget to pay for a yogurt at the grocer's and get pinched? What in hell was it? With Lenny you never knew. Two years older than me, he was a good natured but a decidedly eccentric man who carried, at all times, at least a dozen vitamins and supplements on his person. And intelligent, skilled at what he did— an accountant at a large firm, a diligent worker who could focus on a tough task in a single-minded way—but also someone who, on a lunchtime walk, might stop for a chat and end up involved in an hour's conversation with folks sitting on the stoop of a brownstone. For a time I'd been concerned that his absent-mindedness would get him in trouble and judging by this detective's deadpan expression, I worried that day had come.

Martin's voice then took on a muted quality as he switched into what seemed like an attempt at empathy.

"Dr. Strickman, it is my sad duty to inform you that your brother, Leonard, is deceased. Passed away last night, found this morning by a maid who came in to clean. I am very sorry to have to tell you this, but, of course, you would want to know. His body is now at the morgue and we will need you to identify it."

Lenny dead? I felt a shock rip through my chest. Then numbness. I had heard what he said, but rejected it. I did not believe it. He had used my brother's name, but there was some mistake; they must have confused Lenny with someone else, another Leonard.

Lenny gone? Impossible that my big brother, was gone, had left us. The detective's words, "Your brother, Leonard, is deceased," came back to me, caused a knife to rip through my guts. My eyes burned, began to tear. Never seeing Lenny again, never again being with him sharing family stories, childhood memories. Just the thought left me bereft, empty. Lenny was part of me, part of us, a necessity in our lives.

I relied on him, we all did, the daydreaming bachelor, to show up an hour late for our frequent get-togethers but never to forget a child's birthday. Sometime on that special day he would appear—you never knew when—bearing a clumsily wrapped gift along with a blank birthday card on which, regardless of the honoree, he wrote the same message; 'wishing you a year of good health and good cheer. Your affectionate Uncle Leonard.'

"There has got to be a mistake here," I shouted, "some crazy mix-up. I've heard about these things. You guys make mistakes. You misidentify someone, confuse him with someone else, and drive people crazy."

I was now on my feet, behind my desk, leaning forward, speaking sharply.

"There is nothing wrong with my brother," I barked. "We saw him just last week. He was fine, better than fine. The man sees half a dozen doctors. Just a few days ago I told him how good he looked, that I'd like to be in his shape. He likes his work and loves being with the kids, teaching them, being a mentor. And he takes good care of himself. He is a bit of a hypochondriac."

Martin looked at me as though I were a child having a temper tantrum. He waited for my outburst to end.

"We're not speaking of a health problem, doctor," he said. "not a physical problem."

"What do you mean?"

"It appears that your brother took his own life."

"That's impossible," I blurted out. "Totally crazy. We saw Lenny last week. He was fine, no depression, nothing like that. In fact, I'd say he was in a better mood than I'd seen him in some time, talking about a trip to Israel and taking along one of the kids he works with. No way he could have killed himself."

"Are you telling us that you believe your brother could have been murdered, Doctor?"

"That's insane. No one would want to kill Lenny. He was a thoroughly good man. And nothing wrong with him. He was mentally sound. So if what you are telling me is true, that my brother is dead and he didn't do himself in, someone else had to have done it."

Detective Martin looked at his partner. They exchanged glances, and with a slight movement of her head, she nodded.

"We've considered that, Doctor," Martin said," considered it seriously. An unexplained sudden death does raise questions. So, we are always on the look-out for foul play. It's the first thing we want to rule out.

"So when I explain to you what we've learned and what we believe happened, you'll understand why this was not a homicide."

I waited. I couldn't imagine what he was going to say.

"Are you familiar with the Hotel Pearl, near the Yankee Stadium, the hotel your brother frequented?"

I thought I'd misheard. What in the fucking world was he talking about? In the past decade Lenny had checked into a hotel exactly twice; once in Cleveland for a friend's wedding and once in Rochester for a cousin's Bar Mitzvah. Lenny was total homebody. Traveling to Jersey City for a Seder was as far as he ever wanted to go.

"I'm not following you, Detective," I said. Nothing he was saying made sense.

"Sorry," he replied, "The thing is, Doctor, your brother did not die at home. He was at the hotel I mentioned, the Pearl. One of the maids found him at noon today. In the bathroom. That's where he took his life."

Whatever he was talking about I could not connect in any way with the brother I knew and loved.

Detective Belker then stepped in. She had been standing next to Martin, listening, observing me, content to let him do the talking. But now she intervened.

"Doctor, I have the impression that you are not aware of your brother's situation," she said. "I mean his private life. Am I right about that?"

What the hell was this woman was talking about? She paused and looked at Martin, who then took over. He then proceeded slowly.

"It appears that your brother was one of those men who live two lives," he began, "I gather you knew nothing about this."

I shook my head. I could feel my heart speeding up. I had no idea what to expect.

"I don't know how much of a surprise this is to you, Doctor, but your brother had a secret gay life. That is where the Pearl comes in. He used it to meet men. I'm talking about young guys, the hustlers who hang around those places. We spoke to the manager. Your brother was well known, a regular, he'd been coming for years. They knew his routine. He'd check in about once a month and arrange for one of the hookers to come to his room. Usually he'd stay the night and leave next morning. Never any trouble, never a disturbance of any kind. He came and went and that was it. Except for this last visit. He checked in yesterday, spent the night, and never checked out. Normally he leaves at about 10:00a.m. This morning he didn't appear. All morning, no one saw him. Finally, about noon one of the maids entered his room and found him in the bathtub with a lamp cord around his neck. Used it to hang himself. He attached it to a ceiling fixture but it didn't hold and his body fell into the tub. By time the cord came loose, he was gone. No sign of life when the girl found him."

Martin paused. He was watching me, and when he spoke I heard concern in his voice.

"I'm sorry to be the one to tell you all of this," he said. "I know what it's like to hear such news. But of course you 'd want to know."

I nodded. "I understand, Detective," I said, feeling whiplashed.

But I understood nothing. All I was aware of was a sharp pain in my abdomen, as though Martin had smashed me in the gut.

I saw them watching me, waiting for me to respond, but nothing came. Martin's words now echoed in my head, his voice without emotion, just laying out the facts of the case. Leonard, he had said, was a gay man who had lived a secret life and had done so for years. Sometime last night he had walked into a hotel bathroom, wrapped a lamp cord around his neck, and hanged himself. And no doubt about the cause of death. He'd taken his own life.

"We see cases like this fairly often," Martin was now saying, "two, three times a year. Next to overdosing, this is probably the second most common way people do themselves in"

Listening, I had the feeling that this was experience talking. His presentation was clear, concise, and compelling. I found myself persuaded by the evidence he cited.

But I also knew that he was wrong, that regardless of evidence and logic, what he was telling me could not be true. I sensed the police had rushed to judgment, saw what they saw in front of them, and had drawn a conclusion. But they were wrong. They had overlooked the most important evidence; Lenny himself.

I knew him better than anyone in the world, knew how much our family meant to him, how much I meant to him; knew how loyal he was. He had been very close to our parents, dependent on them, and when they were gone his need for attachment shifted to me and my family. And I'd seen nothing in him to suggest that he was suicidal. Even if I was wrong, even if he had managed to conceal his true feelings and had become despairing about his life—I did not know about his gayness—I was dead certain Lenny would never just abandon us, never leave this earth without a word of explanation. He would have felt a need to share the feelings that compelled him to do this.

Lenny had seen firsthand the toll suicide takes on families, how devastated the survivors are, how they are left with life-long feelings of guilt. My brother would never have done that to us. That I knew.

And it took long, close experience with Lenny to understand who he really was, to know what I knew. Surveying the scene of a death, inspecting the body, examining what other evidence there was, or wasn't; such police work could not tell the true story.

And no note. I checked with Martin and he confirmed that this was so. To make sure—he sensed how important this was to me—he now called the evidence room at headquarters. No note had been found. No recording, photographs, or other visual material. Nothing.

This reinforced my belief, but I saw no use talking about it. I knew these people would never hear me. So with what I knew about my brother and with no one else who knew him to back me up, I was alone. I was furious with these cops who came across as so damn sure of themselves. But I said nothing. I knew if I said anything about the fact that they had no knowledge of Lenny as a person, they would be quick to point out that, in fact, there was quite a bit I did not know about my brother, his homosexual liaisons, for starters.

It was not, in fact, accurate to say that I was totally unaware of Lenny's gayness. Denial, willful blindness, not wanting to deal with knowing; these were closer to the truth.

On several occasions my wife, Alice and I had talked about the possibility that Lenny was a closeted gay, but in the end we concluded that more likely he was one of those asexual men—there are more than you imagine—who have little interest in a sexual life of any kind and for whatever reason lack libido.

Lenny never spoke about sex, never joked about it, and was obviously embarrassed if anyone else did. He had buddies, cronies, mostly fellow congregants from his synagogue, but no one who could be said to be a boyfriend, much less a lover. His passion seemed to be wholly for learning, for Torah study, for his Judaism and, especially, for Israel and its welfare. To organizations that supported those goals, he was generous with both time and money.

Martin by now must have sensed my reluctance to accept his view of my brother's death. And without saying anything, he reached into a back pocket and withdrew a small leather-bound notepad.

"I thought you might want to hear what our Chief is reporting," he offered, "Chief Steiner. He's been on the job thirty-five years. He's seen everything. In a situation like this he likes to inspect the scene, look over everything himself, make sure we've got it right. He came to the hotel a couple of hours after he got the word. He heard the story, inspected the body, looked over everything in the room and dictated his report. I took it down. It's preliminary, a first impression, but it's from the horse's mouth. So, look, I'll read it to you so you'll know what the Chief is submitting. Martin flipped open his notepad and gave a small cough. Then he read.

'Upon preliminary examination at the scene of the death, we find no evidence of criminal activity. There is no evidence of forced entry or attempted robbery. The body appears clean. No blood or bruising on the face or hands, no defensive wounds or signs of a struggle. The body was discovered this morning in a bathtub with a lamp cord around its neck. All signs point to suicide by hanging. A final report will be issued when the results of the postmortem examination are received.'

"That's it," Martin said. "That's how he saw it. Straightforward, if you know what I mean."

Yes, I knew. The Chief umpire had made the call and now no point in pursuing the matter. But what Steiner had not said was also clear. The police now had no intention of investigating Lenny's death beyond routine checking. Unless something unexpected turned up, the case would soon be closed.

Martin looked at me. He could tell that I was not happy with this on-the-spot assessment.

"The Chief didn't mean to give the impression that there was nothing more to be done," he put in quickly. "So, I'd like you to give me the names of anyone outside the family who knew your brother well. We'll contact them, see if they can shed any light on his recent state of mind. And we'll check out his apartment for any relevant material; bills, debts, IOUs, anything like that."

This sounded to me like routine checking, with no expectation of anything coming of it.

So, I did not respond. Clearly nothing to be gained now.

Detective Belker, seeing my expression, and apparently concerned that I might start up again with her partner, stepped in.

"I believe we mentioned that we'll need you to identify the body," she said. "Would you be available to do that?"

"When did you have in mind?"

"Actually now, if that's possible."

Last thing I wanted to do now was to see my brother lifeless on an examining table at the morgue. I was feeling a gnawing pain in my gut as it bore in on me that I would never again see him alive, never again be able to tease him when he arrived for one of our family dinners, late as usual, toting his signature gifts; a ten dollar bottle of wine taken from the cache of weekly specials that he kept in his pantry, and, for our kids, a book, usually about some wonder of nature, inscribed, as always, 'Good reading from your affectionate Uncle Leonard.'

Having now to view his body, to see him actually dead, lined up with a handful of corpses, mostly criminals and street people, to look at his face, drawn and discolored as faces are in death, when they raised the covering sheet just enough for me to see; I felt I could not bear that.

But I also knew, no choice. To put off, as next of kin, what I was obligated to do and to live on in fear of making that dreaded trip; that would be even greater torture.

"All right," I said, "I'll come now. But let's make this as fast as possible."

A patrol car was parked outside. Treating me like a guest, Martin opened the rear door for me, then offered an arm to lean on as I climbed in.

It took under twenty minutes to reach the City Morgue, which was near the courts in lower Manhattan. We rode in silence except for a moment when Detective Belker turned to ask how I was doing.

"I'm alright," I said, "but I'm not looking forward to this."

She nodded. "There's no harder job," she said. "It's the worst. But it won't take long. We'll have you home within the hour."

And she was as good as her word. The identification went quickly. As we approached the morgue she called ahead and when we arrived all was prepared. Near the entrance an attendant was standing alongside a table that held the body. When Martin gave the signal, he lifted the sheet, raising it just high enough for me to see my brother's face. I barely looked. I could not bear more than a quick glance. I had seen my share of corpses during my medical training, and I did not want to remember Lenny as I remembered the faces of those dead; eerily pale, their features drawn and distorted, zombie-like. A glimpse of his dear, familiar brow, the receding hairline, was enough. I nodded. The sheet was lowered and Detective Martin took my arm and led me out.

They then drove me home. Martin walked me to my front door, gave me his card, and asked me to call if I obtained any additional information. In turn, he would be in touch with me when the final report was ready. We shook hands and, to be reassuring, he added a final note.

"We are not going to jump the gun on this case, Doctor," he said. "We'll take our time, talk to people, review everything. Steiner has his opinions, but he can be flexible. If new information turns up, he'll reopen the case. The report we file is not always the last word, if you know what I mean."

"I do," I said. I got his message.

He was preparing me for the fact that the report would contain the official police determination of the cause of my Lenny's death: suicide by hanging. I thanked him for his efforts and told him that I would be in touch. Then I let myself in.

For the next two hours I sat with Alice, and we talked. I told her everything, every detail, from Linda's knock on my office door to the final handshake with Martin. I also needed to make my case with her, to convince her that the police were wrong, that they erred because they made the mistake of diagnosing the scene, not the person, and if they had known Lenny they could not have believed that he'd taken his own life.

Alice was a keen observer and she'd seen Lenny just the week before when he had been at our house for dinner. I expected her to second everything I said; to be in total agreement with me.

But she wasn't.

"We knew your brother as well as anyone," she said, "and the truth is we knew very little about him, about the private person. He always kept his guard up, let you in on so much and no more. And what he didn't want you to know, you had no chance of ever finding out. He was masterful at concealing his sexuality. So, no reason to think he hadn't done the same with his moods. Lenny knew how to wear a mask. He could have been depressed for years—God knows he had reason enough to be—and hid it so well when he was with us that we never recognized what he might be going through."

She then pointed out that my thinking was flawed in another way, too. She agreed that Lenny would never have taken his own life without so much as a word of explanation to us, but she challenged my statement that he had left no suicide message of any kind.

"You've got blinders on, Bill," she said. "All you see is what sits squarely in front of your nose. You are telling me that if the cops didn't find a note on the body or in the hotel room, that means there was none. But what if the note is sitting on his kitchen table or right now is traveling through the US mails? You've been watching too many crime shows, Bill. Whenever they depict a suicide, the note is always on the body or right nearby. But Lenny was an original. He didn't follow scripts. Maybe he sent his note UPS and it will arrive tomorrow."

And she was right. I simply had assumed that if my brother had committed suicide, his note would be near the body as on Law and Order it always is. It never occurred to me that it could be someplace else. So much for my ability to think outside the TV box. How much of the human brain, I wondered, has been co-opted by media images that swamp it from the moment of birth.

I pulled myself up and headed for the door.

"I'll be back in an hour. Please hold dinner."

"Where are you going?"

"To Lenny's apartment. If you're right and he left a message for me, I need to see it before the police. There could be something in it that he did not want anyone else to see."

"Like what?"

"I have no idea. Perhaps a confession of some kind, something only for us, or who knows, maybe something else."

"Like what else?"

I could not respond. A frightening thought had come into my head. Finally, I spoke.

"Like the name of his murderer."

Lenny lived in a garden apartment in Riverdale, fifteen-minute drive from my house in Teaneck. He'd been there for years, a two-bedroom, thoroughly undistinguished flat that had not been graced with a coat of paint for more than a decade. And then it was only at Alice's insistence years ago that Lenny had agreed to the painting of two rooms on the condition that they remain the same steel grey color that he was used to.

A number of Lenny's cronies, all members of the local Orthodox Shul, had done well in business and had moved into those steel and glass high rises, complete with gyms and pools that had sprung up in his neighborhood. Lenny was not tempted to follow suit. He had no interest in more light and space; still less in modern design or the amenities that the new buildings offered. He liked to settle into the large blue armchair that dominated his smallish living room, switch on the decades-old brass lamp that stood alongside his chair, and lose himself in Torah readings or the latest book by a political pundit on possible solutions to the Middle East conflict. In the latter case, he would keep a red marker at the ready so as to write comments in the margins and give vent to his indignation at the author's wrong-headed statements, many of which had to do with his failure to appreciate the extent of the threat to Israel posed by the growing military strength of its hostile Arab neighbors.

I had a key and let myself in. What struck me immediately was the odor of decaying flowers. Lenny loved flower arranging, and before he left a couple of days earlier, he had filled a blue vase with a spring bouquet, expecting, no doubt, to enjoy it upon his return.

Before anything else, I disposed of the dying flowers. Then I turned to the task at hand; a quick, but thorough, search of all four rooms, focusing on any and all places where my brother might have left a letter or note for me.

The job was easy. Lenny was a neat freak. He kept his apartment in immaculate condition. Anything out of order caused him anxiety, so he was diligent about tidying up and keeping his possessions in their assigned places.

So, it took me less than a half hour to do a though search. I examined everything; desk, tables, shelves, closets, drawers, all of it. And found nothing. Or almost nothing. Just prior to leaving, I decided to do a check of the small second bedroom that Lenny used as his study. I had searched three vertical drawers on the right side of his desk and found nothing, but on second look I noticed a small drawer on the opposite side, its surface blending so seamlessly with the wood grain that it was almost imperceptible.

Inside I found a few sheets of paper stapled together. I glanced at them. They seemed to be the transcript of a radio talk on Middle East affairs. The words, policies, resistances, brutality, Intifada caught my eye as did the names, Netanyahu and Hamas. I imagined that the broadcast had interested Lenny, as did almost any commentary on the Middle East conflict, and that he had sent for this transcript. Either that or one of his cronies had heard the program, had gotten hold of it, and sent it on to him.

Whatever its source, this material, although possibly interesting in itself, had nothing to do with what I was looking for. And by then I was eager to get home and not take the time to read this script. But I was curious as to what it was that caused Lenny to keep a copy, so I slipped the pages into an empty folder and took it with me.

My thought was to read it at home. I pictured reclining in my favorite armchair, the script in front of me, and as I read, experiencing my brother sitting alongside me, looking over my shoulder, waiting for me to finish so that we could discuss—and debate—the speaker's contentions.

While searching, I was totally preoccupied with my task and had given no thought to the impact on me of being alone in my brother's home, where once a month, I sat with him, drank tea, and discussed a passage from the Talmud.

On the way home, though, I suddenly felt overcome with sadness. Waves of grief tore at my insides, bore into them, and left a residue of dull pain

But I was relieved that I had found no suicide note, no communication of that kind, which meant that Lenny had not taken his own life. I knew in my heart that he would never have left without an explanation, to those he loved.

And, I also felt bereft, cheated that there was no last word from him, no good-bye, no contact. Just silence and emptiness.

And my finding nothing now brought me face to face with something impossible; murder. Someone had taken my brother's life. I could see no other explanation. And yet the idea that someone had murdered Lenny, had come into his hotel room, wrapped a lamp cord around his neck, and hanged him, was so wild a notion, so alien, that when, at home, I spoke of it to Alice, I felt as though I was describing the outlandish plot of a trashy novel.

What then took place in my own living room, however, was also right up there on the incredulity scale. It was as unexpected, as inexplicable, as the idea of the murder itself.

Within an hour of returning home, not only did I have in my possession information that supported the idea of murder, but evidence that pointed to a suspect. What complicated matters, however, was that the person it pointed to was someone I knew to be incapable of killing anyone; had no capacity, morally, ethically, or in any way to do so.

The transcript consisted of a critique of Orthodox Jews for their blind support of the right wing, anti-Arab Israeli government, and their refusal to acknowledge that its policies violated the spirit and meaning of Judaism, with its insistence on righteous behavior and concern for one's fellow man.

And, to my amazement, my brother was singled out as an example of just this willful blindness, a Jew devoted to his religion and its values who, nevertheless, refused to recognize the inhumanity of Israel's behavior toward its neighbors, its brutal and punitive occupation of the Palestinian homeland. He was, in short, a hypocrite.

And scrawled in the margins was Lenny's response, his counterattack. "Vicious lies," he wrote, "slanderous, anti-Semitic," and, as his final shot, his summing up; "a pathetic effort to cover up."

All this struck me as incomprehensible. What in the world was it about? From the author's style, his phrasing, as well as his familiar themes, I knew who he was. I'd had long experience battling him, contending with his persuasiveness, the cleverness of his arguments. But I had no idea that he even knew my brother. I'd had no hint they had ever crossed paths.

The writer of this stinging critique was Dr. Ahmed Aslam, who, it turned out, not only knew my brother, but, as I discovered, had reason to wish him transported to another world.

A Palestinian whose family fled to Lebanon when Israel invaded Gaza, Ahmed had been teacher, mentor, friend and longtime adversary of mine. I first met him when, as a green tomato of an intern, I was assigned to our hospital's trauma service where he was the attending physician.

Early on, I recognized how gifted a surgeon Ahmed was, without question the most dedicated and skillful one on the staff. From him I learned all that I came to know about handling trauma; knifings, gunshot wounds, crushing injuries, often the result of gang fights—our hospital was in the roughest part of the Lower East Side—that had turned deadly.

In dealing with patients, Ahmed focused on a single goal; the preservation of life. It was not rare for him to log eight, ten, a dozen hours at a stretch in the OR, all the time on his feet, all the time laboring to repair the ravaged body of an unknown street kid, someone whom the Emergency Room doctors had declared unsalvageable.

In some respects, we couldn't have been more different, Ahmed and I; teacher and student, expert and novice, Arab and Jew, natural antagonists when it came to our views as to which of our people brought on the never-ending agony of the Israel-Palestinian struggle.

Hardly a day went by that we did not go at it, often drawing spectators eager to see the bullfight. But our fights did not affect our fondness for one another. Against all reason, we formed a bond, a closeness that neither of us understood but that developed, perhaps, because what we cared about, what meant most to us, at base, was very much the same.

It was not unusual, after one of our knockdown-drag-outs, for us to retreat to the doctor's lounge, sip coffee, and review the approaches that Ahmed had developed to deal with his most serious cases; penetrating abdominal wounds, the result of a bullet or thrusting knife, and the crushing chest injuries, often the sequelae of a vengeful attack by an enraged individual who had used a car or truck as a deadly weapon.

After I left that service, we kept up contact, seeing one another every couple of weeks, drinking, arguing, and enjoying one another's company. When, for some reason, I did not see Ahmed for a month or two, I missed him and would seek him out. He was always responsive, glad to see me, always ready to reminisce, recall our days together. Until he wasn't; until he disappeared, vanished, leaving behind a wound, a rawness in me that I felt as a low-level pain that did not heal.

In the course of our debates, I came to know Ahmed's arguments well; his contention that for their own selfish reasons, the Israelis had driven his people from their historic lands and now kept them secluded, choked off, forced to live stunted lives by a brutal occupation.

This message he was ready to deliver to anyone who would listen—a number of doctors hid out when they saw him coming—and he also had a monthly radio program to support his cause.

On occasion, he attacked individuals who opposed him. Since some of those were allies of mine, I knew exactly who he was critiquing. What I couldn't figure was not only why he had come after my brother, but how he knew him at all.

What seemed likely was this situation came about as a consequence of two brothers keeping secrets; not one secret shared between Lenny and myself, but two identical secrets that we kept from one another.

For our own reasons, neither of us acknowledged knowing Ahmed, not to mention each of us having a complex, often fraught, relationship with him.

I never told my brother about Ahmed because I knew there would be endless questions. Who is he, what is his religion, his politics, his attitude toward Israel and the Jews? And what made me choose to be involved with an Arab anyway? Lenny would never say it openly, but he didn't have to. For him, a friendship between two people from mutually hostile societies who have been fed hatred of the other along with their mother's milk, can never endure; sooner or later the strains will show and, the friends—in this case Arab and Jew—will turn against one another.

But the origin of Lenny's secret was different. However he got to know Ahmed—I had yet to find out—he would have discovered that Ahmed and I had a long-standing friendship. And given the antipathy that had developed between himself and Ahmed, Lenny would not have wanted to put me in the middle, to make me choose and end up a loser. no matter who I chose. That's who Lenny was; always considerate, always thinking of the other guy.

But I was curious to know how Lenny and Ahmed had met and what led to open warfare. And more than curious, I sensed that understanding what happened between them could well be the key to unlocking the mystery of my brother's death.

For the second time I turned to the transcript in the hope of finding some answers.

And I found them, a few sentences that gave me an angle, a pathway to follow, even if for some time I was convinced it was a blind alley.

It was on the last page that I noticed a few lines in my brother's hand, scrawled and almost illegible. I had to hold it close to my face to make anything of it.

When I managed to decipher the words, a wave of excitement came over me; excitement, mixed with fear and an urge to hide what I had just found. Lenny's words now made clear his resolve to strike back at Ahmed, to make him pay for his attack

"This *momsa* doesn't know what is in store for him," my brother wrote, "him and his *gonif* friends. What I have, the proof, is going to give these Jew haters what they deserve."

That was it, all there was. But this was not mere name-calling. This also was an openly stated threat. My brother had something on Ahmed, something that presumably posed a real threat to him. Whether this had to do with a criminal act or something else, Lenny hadn't said. But what he knew had to be important enough for its exposure to be seriously damaging. For an immigrant like Ahmed, that could mean expulsion from the U.S., or even prison time.

I am no detective, but in my work I am often faced with puzzles; how, for instance, did a patient of mine get herself into such a tangle of impossible relationships? In such situations, I find it useful to reconstruct each of the steps that took her to this unhappy place.

So now I set out to do the same thing; try to reconstruct the steps that led to my brother's death.

The first question Had to be the meeting between Lenny and Ahmed. How and where this happened, I did not know, but somewhere along the line the two got entangled. That friction was likely to develop between them, Arab and Jew, ardent Zionist and indefatigable advocate for the Palestinian cause, would have been obvious to anyone who knew them both. Also, now evident, was that this clash had reached a boiling point.

So Ahmed then launched his attack, and in retaliation, Lenny made clear his intention to expose Ahmed for serious wrongdoing.

For someone in Ahmed's vulnerable position, this threat would have constituted a danger that had to be eliminated.

And now, following this exchange of insults and threats, my brother is found dead in a hotel bathroom with a lamp cord around his neck.

I don't know if Chief Steiner would have regarded this series of events as solid evidence or merely as suggestive of a suspect; someone who could have reason to want Leonard Strickman eliminated.

To Alice, though, the scenario I put together was compelling. It permitted only one conclusion: my old friend had murdered my brother.

Alice's thinking was based both on the sequence of steps which had an inexorable quality, a steady building toward this inevitable denouement, and on a subtext that, for her, was the hidden, but powerful, motive for my brother's murder.

To Ahmed, she pointed out, Lenny was not only a hateful Zionist who blindly followed the dictates of the Israeli religious right. Unconsciously he represented the iconic Jew, the Jew who had driven the Palestinians from their homeland and had inflicted terrible pain on those Ahmed loved. He was the persecutor, the Jew who was responsible for the subjugation of the Arab people.

I followed her thinking, appreciated her understanding of depth psychology, and recognized that most of what she said was true. Except for one flaw. She did not know Ahmed the way I knew him. I spend my working life trying to understand peoples' characters, seeking to explore what lies behind the shields they put up. And I take pride in being pretty good at what I do.

I had logged a ton of time with Ahmed Aslam, spent hours with him in and out of the OR. I knew him as a healer, a preserver of life, a physician committed to honoring his Hippocratic Oath; First, do no harm.

Everything I knew about him told me there was no way he could take the life of another human being.

I thought it best to keep this belief to myself. But I didn't. I found myself saying that there was more to this than Alice thought; that she was operating on logic, rationality, the physical facts as she knew them. But reason, facts, logic do not always tell the whole story. Her account left out something essential; Ahmed, the man. Understanding him, one would also understand that her logical conclusion was, in fact, a red herring. Ahmed could not be a murderer.

Alice's response was measured, but contained a hint of impatience at my not grasping the obvious.

"The Ahmed you are talking about no longer exists," she said. "That man is long gone. The person who answers to that name today is a total stranger, and since we now know that he's joined some militant group, it's highly likely that this Ahmed has now been programmed to kill."

Alice was referring to some news about Ahmed that had circulated in the hospital community a couple of years after he disappeared. Word had it that he had undergone a radical conversion, endorsed the thinking and philosophy of certain revolutionary groups, and, in fact, had aligned himself with one committed to the idea that only force could produce change.

I had no idea if what we had heard about Ahmed was true. At first, I doubted it. It seemed the kind of rumor circulated by certain doctors, primarily those he vanquished in debates. These thoroughly disliked him, labeled him anti-Semite, and did all they could to besmirch his reputation.

On reflection, though, I came to think that what we heard about him was entirely possible, that living among his people, many of whom were displaced Palestinians, and witnessing how marginal their lives now were, how limited and void of hope, he could have come to believe, as had the American Colonists some two hundred years before him, that the only way forward was revolution. I could see that as a possibility. At base Ahmed, the Ahmed I knew, was an idealist.

"I don't know if you've followed what happens to the converts who join these militant groups," Alice was saying, "but they became transformed. They are brain washed, manipulated, fed hateful propaganda, and turned into killers. Many become the bomb carriers who end up with their body parts strewn among those of the innocent people they have slaughtered.

"Over here we have no real understanding of these jihadist types, who they are, what drives their zeal. But one thing we do know is not to underestimate their power to distort minds. If your friend, Ahmed, is involved with one of those groups, you can bet that he's learned to kill."

I knew that in most respects Alice was right. What I had heard about the way young Muslim men from slum areas in England and elsewhere are trained to destroy the enemies of Allah, the non-believers, Jews and Christians alike, made clear that anyone, once in the hands of these radical Islamists, would be manipulated into pledging to carry out jihad; to eradicate infidels, wherever they were.

And it is true, I thought, that the power of such groups is enormous. Over the years, I'd encountered patients who, in one-to-one situations were capable of asserting their views and holding their own, but who were unable to withstand the pressure of a group; strong individuals who, in that situation, lost their assertiveness and became followers.

I knew Ahmed only in a one to one setting, I had no idea how he would behave in a group. Nonetheless, something in me, some deep feeling, an irrational need of some kind, caused me to hold to the view that Ahmed Aslam, could not be a killer.

Alice contended that under intense group pressure and fear for one's life, anyone could kill. I disagreed. A great many, perhaps the majority, would succumb, I argued, but some, for reasons of character, conviction, or deep-seated obstinacy, would not. Ahmed, to me, was one of those.

I realized, though, that I might be dead wrong, that I might be indulging in wishful thinking, a trait of mine with which Alice was thoroughly familiar.

So I was totally confused. I no longer knew if what I believed was true or whether I just needed it to be that way. And that now included my conviction that my brother had not taken his own life. Perhaps the police were right after all. I began to think that I might have rejected Steiner's verdict simply because I could not accept that reality. That perhaps was the hard truth.

All I knew for certain was that I needed help, needed someone who could make sense of all of this, a professional person with clear vision who had been in situations like this before and knew how to carry out a skilled investigation,

I needed a Philip Marlow of my own, someone who had been around the block a few times, who could look beyond the obvious and sniff out the truth in this baffling situation.

But who could that be? I knew no one who remotely fit that description. The kind of detectives I knew worked in analysts' offices and were limited to ferreting out unconscious Oedipal and incestuous fantasies.

As for private investigators, what I'd heard about them made me wary. They sounded like an odd bunch, mostly former law enforcement people trying to augment their retirement pay. Few of these, I imagined, were up to carrying out a challenging murder investigation and I did not want to make a blind choice that ended up draining my bank account and yielding very little.

To quell the anxiety I was experiencing, I took to my bed, fell asleep, and had a short dream. In it I am treating a troubled adolescent whose first name begins with the letter, G. Upon awakening, I sensed that the dream was trying to tell me something, but I had no idea what. I gave it a good deal of thought, tried to decipher the dream's concealed message, but came up with nothing. Then, all at once, just as I was about to abandon the effort, a man's name appeared in my mind: Barney Siegal. And then, I understood.

Barney Siegal was a cop at the 23rd precinct. Ten years ago, he came to me in desperation. His adolescent son, Gregory, had gotten himself into a barrel full of trouble. On impulse he had stolen an expensive camera from an electronics store, had been caught and arrested, and now faced felony charges. If convicted, he might well go to jail and, in his father's view, his life would be ruined. It turned out that Gregory was suffering from bipolar illness and the theft was carried out while he was in a manic phase. I took the boy into treatment, he was given a suspended sentence, and with the help of therapy and medication, he did extremely well. He stabilized, excelled in school, and gained admission to a prestigious college.

Deeply grateful, Barney wanted to give me an expensive gift. I thankfully declined, and reassured him that simply having the opportunity to work with his son and see him make such great strides was gift enough.

"No, it's not," Barney insisted. "You saved my son's life. I've seen what happens to people who've been convicted as felons. They can never shake that label. No matter what else they do, people think of them as criminals. The label sticks and ultimately it destroys their lives. Look doctor," he continued, "I understand that you can't take gifts. But I want you to make me a promise. If you ever need police help to handle a speeding ticket, get a gun permit, provide protection from a mad patient, or, God forbid, a furious wife, anything at all, you'll call on me. Day or night. It doesn't matter. I'll be there for you."

I thanked Barney, and duly promised to call if I needed him, but also expressed hope that I would never have to ask him to make good on his offer. Then I forgot about the whole exchange.

Now it all came back. I could call in my marker and contact Barney Siegal. I had no idea if he was still around and, if he was, whether he would remember me. And even if he did and wanted to help, how helpful could someone like that be? After all, he was a policeman, a plain vanilla cop, not a crack detective. Nonetheless, I had a hunch that Barney could be helpful. The man had been around for a long time. He had been dealing with criminals for decades and he'd seen just about every crime in the book. He might have some fresh ideas and, and in any case, there was nothing to lose. At the least, he could help me make some useful contacts, set me on the right path.

I went to a storage cabinet at the rear of my office, located the old rotating index card file that I had used a decade ago, found Barney's number, and feeling a surprising jolt of anxiety in my gut, made the call.

Chapter 2

The cop who answered the phone at the 23rd had no idea who I was talking about.

"Barney Siegal?" There is no one here by that name."

"I know he used to be at your precinct. I've reached him there in the past."

"At the 23rd? You're sure you have that right?

"Quite sure."

"Must have been before my time. I tell you what. If you hang on, sir, I'll ask the captain. He's been around forever. He has the whole history of the NYPD in his head."

"Thanks. I'll wait."

Ten minutes later the desk officer's voice came back on.

"Barney Siegal retired four years ago. He's in Connecticut now. I have the number. You can probably reach him there if he hasn't passed on by now."

"Let's hope not. I'll try anyway."

I made the call as soon as I hung up. A vaguely familiar voice came on the line.

"Barney Siegal here. Who is calling?"

"Mr. Siegal, this is Dr. William Strickman. I don't know if you remember me. I treated your son Gregory, about ten years ago."

"Do you think I could *ever* forget such a thing, Doctor? You performed a miracle and I'm not one to forget miracles. It's not our lot to experience many of those in a lifetime. I can attest to that."

"How is your son doing?"

"He's a CPA, if you can believe that. This is a boy who couldn't pass 5th grade math. He's working with a big New York firm and leading the bachelor life. On track to make partner, so he tells me."

"That's wonderful news."

"And you, Doctor, how are you and yours?"

"Doing well, thank you. We're good."

"And to what do I owe the honor of this call?"

"I don't know if you will remember this, Mr. Siegal, but at our last meeting you offered your services should I ever need your help. Well, I need your help now. I hope that time has not run out on your offer."

"I remember that very well, Doctor, and no, there is no time limit on an offer from Barney Siegal. I am delighted that you called. How can I be of help?"

It's a complex matter. I can't really explain it over the phone. Can we make a date to talk in person? I'd be glad to come to you if you tell me where you live."

"We're outside Hartford, near my sister's family. But you just sit tight, Doctor, I'll be at your door at ten o'clock tomorrow morning."

"There's no need for you to make that trip. I can easily drive up."

"Actually, there is a need. It's my need, and I won't have it any other way. If you'll have a cup of coffee ready, that would be splendid."

"It's a deal. And thank you. I'll be expecting you at ten tomorrow"

"It will be my pleasure."

That call triggered memories. I recalled qualities of Barney's that struck me as odd. At times he would refer to himself in the third person, saying something like 'Barney Siegel had this or that thought.' At first

I regarded this as a piece of pomposity—a king might speak of himself this way—but I discovered that it represented something else; an effort on Barney's part to stand back and see himself objectively, to view Barney Siegel from the outside, as it were. Peculiar as it was, this was his attempt at self-assessment.

Once I got used to this oddity, I found it admirable, as I did Barney's ability, not so common in the parents I worked with, to shoulder his share of the blame for his son's difficulties.

"I didn't see what was happening and I didn't want to see it." Barney told me, "Greg was my son. He was supposed to be perfect, a showpiece for what a great dad I was."

And Barney had keen insight into his boy's difficulties. He understood that Greg's theft of a camera conveyed his belief that he deserved reparations for being unfairly afflicted with an illness that caused him to be shunned by his peers.

I had not thought of Barney Siegel for years before I had the dream, but there was something about him, a quirkiness, a unique Barney way of seeing things, that must have led me to think that he could approach the puzzle of Lenny's death with fresh eyes, come up with a new angle, and initiate a search for the truth.

At five minutes to ten the next morning the doorbell rang and I was confronted with a person I would not have recognized if I ran straight into his huge belly. I remembered Barney Siegal as a big man, but now his expansion—in all directions—made him seem a cartoon caricature of himself.

"Yogurt's the culprit," Barney announced when he caught sight of the expression on my face. "Frozen yogurt. It's my waterloo. My doctor claims it is healthier than ice cream, so I switched and you see the result. No offense, Doctor, but I blame the medical profession. Of course, as my wife reminds me, the good doctor did not prescribe a quart of strawberry yogurt at bedtime, but that is beside the point. We live near a yogurt stand, so my wife won't let me out of the house alone. I am starting a twelve-step program, Yogurt Fressers Anonymous I expect a big turnout."

"I'll be the first to join up," I said. "I'm hooked, too."

"Then we're soul mates, Doctor. I felt the vibrations from the moment we met."

I ushered Barney into my study. After he had settled himself—he filled and overflowed an extra-wide recliner—Alice brought in a carafe of coffee. But as an act of solidarity with Barney's wife, omitted the tray of pastries she had planned to serve.

After we'd drained our cups, I launched into my story. I understood that if he were to be helpful, Barney needed to know everything, so I held nothing back.

He listened like a psychoanalyst, taking in everything and saying nothing. When I'd finished, he sat back, put his fingertips together, and let out a low whistle.

"That is some story, Doctor. I am very sorry about your brother. That is a terrible loss. It sounds as though he had many of your sterling qualities."

"Only a few. But I loved him anyway."

Barney smiled, "Give me a picture, Doc. I need to know Lenny, get a feel for your brother."

"Religious and stubborn for starters. As a teenager he became Orthodox for reasons I never understood. We weren't a religious family, but he found something he needed in religion and he remained observant from then on. We were very different that way. Religion never had that kind of appeal for me, but I respected Lenny's decision and it did not prevent us from being close. We relied on one another a great deal. Whenever I needed him, he was there for me, always ready to listen to my latest problem, always able to say something positive to lift my spirits.

"And I was a kind of seeing eye for him, someone who would help him navigate the world when he needed some direction. I loved my brother deeply but he wasn't the most practical man in the world. He had a way of acting on impulse—he once took on an Anti-Semite fascist-type on Broadway and got a twelve-inch gash on his face for his trouble. And as far as generosity was concerned, he was over the top. He once gave half his savings to a destitute couple who wanted to emigrate to Israel. More than once I had to hold him back from giving away the store."

I had a lot more to say about my brother, but suddenly feelings welled up and I choked and couldn't go on. I tried to excuse myself, but Barney held up a hand. He understood. He was silent for a minute, giving me time to recover. Then he changed the subject.

"I was wondering about something," he said, "the police verdict is suicide, right?"

"According to Steiner."

"Correct me if I'm wrong, Doctor, but isn't suicide forbidden in Orthodox Judaism? Wouldn't that rule out suicide?"

"Unfortunately, no. Lenny was Orthodox, but independent. He did his own thinking and he had his share of fights with the Rabbis. No, if he was determined to kill himself, religion wouldn't have stopped him."

"He was his own man. And feisty, if I get the picture."

"Feisty doesn't do him justice. Lenny could get into arguments seven days a week. Mostly they were Talmudic disputes with his cronies, but also over politics. Lenny was a Zionist and a great defender of the State of Israel. He had a lot of fights with his *Shul* buddies over that, but he never held grudges. He and one of the other *altacockers* could go head to head for hours, but when it was all over, he and the other guy, the putz who my brother had accused of reading the Talmud with his *tush*, would walk down to the corner deli and make peace over bowls of borscht."

"There was no bad blood? Lenny didn't have an enemy who wanted to see him strung up in a hotel john?"

"Nothing like that. He could aggravate the hell out of you with his Talmudic style of disputing, but you couldn't stay mad at the guy. In the end, he always managed to win you over with some thoughtful gesture, and you'd forget that an hour ago you were ready to bash his skull in."

Saying this brought back memories of the little gifts Lenny would buy me—a calendar of the year's Jewish holidays, a souvenir tee shirt from a Matzoh factory he had visited, a movie pass that had been distributed at work—and I felt the tears coming on. I had managed to keep them at bay for a while, but with these memories and feeling again the caring and the love contained in them, they broke through. I looked away but I felt embarrassed and stupid. Why the hell was I letting myself go in front of someone I barely knew? I had no idea who Barney Siegal truly was. Looking at him now, with his pillow-like belly and raspy voice, he reminded me of W.C. Fields minus the alcohol and with a few Yiddish-isms added.

There was something, though, about Barney that drew me to him; a kind of haimish warmth, an openness and ability to reach out, that made you feel that he was on your side. With Barney I soon realized I did not have to be on guard. He was a straight shooter who had no problem letting you know if he thought you were off base—he diagnosed me as a *meshuga* shrink for suggesting the police might be reluctant to spend money investigating the death of an Orthodox Jew—but he was never mean. Meanness was not in Barney Siegal's nature.

"I had a brother, too, Doc," Barney was saying, "younger and a sweetheart. They don't come any better. One of those people who was there for you no matter what. Mac was a teacher of high school English, always quoting Chaucer and Shakespeare. He was on the plane that went down off Long Island. You remember that, Doc? Just took off and plunged into the Atlantic Ocean. He was with his fiancé, their first trip abroad. The two of them must have saved every spare penny in one of those vacation club accounts. How's that for irony, or fate, or whatever you call it.

"My folks were alive then but that put them in their graves. They never recovered. And I nearly joined them. I had to take off a month from the Force and when I came back, I wasn't Barney Siegal. I was someone imitating me. It took me years to get back and I don't think I'm there yet. So, I know what you're going through now, Doctor. You never have to be embarrassed around Barney Siegal."

"Thanks," I said, "I appreciate that."

"One thing, though, before we team up," Barney went on, "I need you to know who I am, who you're signing up with. For thirty-three of my thirty-seven years on the Force I was one of two things; a cop on the street or a cop in a car. I made traffic stops, broke up gang fights, refereed husband-wife quarrels, took strokes and cardiac cases to the hospital. That was pretty much it.

Over the years I took a slew of exams, never got promoted until near the end of my time. Then I made detective. But as far as those boys were concerned, I was already an old dog. I got assigned to purse-snatchers, prostitutes, and naughty street vendors. My specialty was the lowliest crimes on the street. They treated me pretty much like a faithful mascot. So if you are looking for one of those private eyes who spots the missing clue and brings in the bad guy before the last commercial goes on, I'm not your man. On the other hand," he added, "I've been around the block a few times and I've picked up a couple of things. So I might come up with an idea or two."

"That's just what I'm looking for," I replied. "A man with ideas."

"Well the first thing I have to say is the cops are no dummies. Especially Chief Steiner. If Steiner says it's suicide, that carries a lot of weight with the top brass. They'll take his word for it and that will pretty much close the case. So, it will be up to us to prove him wrong."

"From what you say, that's not likely to happen."

"It's a tall order, sure, but nothing's impossible. You know that, Doctor. You take people who are far out, folks barely hanging on, and you bring them back, turn them into *menches*, so you ought to know something about miracle-making."

"Actually, miracles are not in my toolkit," I said, "I'll leave them to those who have a need to believe in such things. What I do know is that what passes for a miracle is ninety-nine percent perspiration and one percent dumb luck."

"We are on the same page, there Doctor. That's exactly what it will take for us to come up with an answer in this case. From what you've said, your brother wasn't the type to do himself in. Which means that someone else took on that little job. Clearly, our friends at Big Blue don't believe that. They're convinced they're dealing with a suicide, so there'll be no help from them. No fingerprints, no DNA collection, no interviewing the hotel staff, nothing. So, when it comes to evidence, we are starting off with *bupkus*, a big zero. All we have is your sense that Steiner and company are on the wrong track. And that's not something we can present to the DA."

I must have looked upset by what Barney was saying, He quickly held up a hand.

"Don't get me wrong Doctor. Your take on what happened to your brother is important. I regard those kinds of things; hunches, gut feelings, as valuable evidence. When I was on the detective squad, I had my radar working twenty-four-seven. And it paid off. I'd be walking out and I'd have a gut feeling that a perp was in the vicinity. Then I'd spot some character in a doorway, and I'd know right off the guy was carrying hot property. Don't ask me how I knew. It's a mystery, some kind of personal radar. Everyone has it, but most people don't use it. They don't realize what a tool they have. If you give it free reign, it will point the way, lead you in the right direction. But you've got to trust it, let it speak for you."

"And is your radar telling you anything now?"

"It's telling me to follow your lead, that you knew your brother and could read him in a way no outsider could. So I say let the boys Downtown think what they like. Let them close the case. For us it's wide open. We'll start our own homicide investigation."

The word, homicide, shocked me. I knew, of course, that if Lenny didn't kill himself and didn't collapse of his own accord, someone else had to have done it. But the idea that anyone would want to murder Lenny remained unthinkable. "It's true his stubbornness could drive you mad," I said to Barney, "in an argument he'd repeat the same point a dozen times. But if he saw he'd upset you, he'd give you a smile or crack a stupid joke and you'd forget how angry you'd just been."

At that point I realized that I hadn't told Barney about the transcript, with its exchanges of insults and Lenny's threat. I feared that information would cause him to focus on Ahmed and I didn't want him to reinforce the idea, which something in me continued to rebel against, that my old friend and mentor was the killer.

Barney understood.

"I went through something like this," he said, "a long time ago. My favorite uncle got drunk, got into a fight with his ex-wife, and stabbed her. She died in the hospital three days later. He cooked up an alibi, got a couple of cronies to say he was with them when it happened, and nearly got away with it. But I knew him.

I knew what a mean drunk he was, and that he'd done it. So I searched his house and found the evidence; a bloody nightgown at the bottom of a recycling bin. My uncle died in prison. It was the toughest thing I ever had to do, but the man took a human life. You can't let a person get away with that, no matter what they mean to you."

I knew he was right, that we had to follow through on Ahmed even though I was sure we'd find out we were barking up the wrong tree. And in any case, we had no live body to investigate. Wherever he was, our suspect was beyond our reach, his whereabouts unknown and, it seemed, unknowable. Ahmed had vanished and all my efforts to find him had turned up nothing.

"At the 23rd did they teach you how to track down a virtual suspect?" I asked.

"He's real enough," Barney said. "You'll point us in the right direction, tell us where to find him. The info we need is in your head."

"How is it that sounds like one of Barney's more imaginative ideas?" I asked.

"Because you haven't taken a dose of your own medicine. You've logged a lot of time with this Ahmed character. Somewhere along the line he's given you clues as to where he's likely to be. Lie down on your couch and do that free association bit. What you know will come back to you."

"I'm touched by your faith in me, partner, but the fact is when it comes to me being the patient and using my own method, I'm afraid you are looking at a rusted-out machine."

"You don't give yourself credit, Doc. You're not through yet. Think of your man, Sigmund. The old guy was still knocking off socks in his eighties. Give it a shot. You may surprise yourself."

"I'll think about it."

Barney was persuasive. After he'd left and we arranged to meet the next day, I retreated to my study, lay down on the couch, and let my mind go. Or tried to. As I suspected, what arose was detritus; thoughts about last night's dinner, my appointment schedule, some O.R. experiences I'd had with Ahmed, but no clues, nothing that pointed a direction.

After a half hour, I gave up. Attempting to free associate was hard work. It had been years since I had been in analysis myself and I had forgotten how much it took out of you, how much of a struggle it is to break through the resistances to knowing itself that the mind puts up.

I turned on the TV. The Giants-Eagles came on. It was half-time and the Maras, owners of the Giants, were receiving an award for their support of the American Cancer Society.

As I watched, a strange thing happened. The face of Tim Mara, an Irish face, became fuller, darker, more swarthy. And as it did, it became the face of Vince Lombardi, the legendary coach of the Green Bay Packers. It was Lombardi who was receiving an award, the coveted Super Bowl trophy.

Odd as this was, clearly an illusion that got me thinking that I needed to return to my old analyst's couch, I knew that this experience was a continuation of my associations; that it was relevant to what I was seeking, if only I could decode the message it contained.

In fact, that did not take long. Associating to the name, Lombardi, supplied the answer. Lombardi led to the name Lombardo, Sally Lombardo, the social worker in charge of volunteers at our hospital.

About a year ago, she helped my brother obtain a volunteer position with disadvantaged children at her favorite agency, the Harlem Youth Center.

And then I recalled something else, that once when we were out drinking, Ahmed had confided that he felt guilty for having fared so much better than his Palestinian friends.

Through connections with Lebanese and Israeli colleagues, his father was able to move the family to Lebanon when Ahmed was twelve. This allowed him to have an education and a life that his old comrades could only dream of. He had become a doctor and a surgeon while they lived marginal existences, forever struggling to find work that would sustain their families.

Ahmed felt a need to pay back, to help his people, but beyond sending money, there was little else he could do from the U.S. He complained a lot about that, but found no other way to show his gratitude for the advantages he had been given.

At one point I told him he was frustrated because he had blinders on.

"Children are children," I said. "There are kids right here who are hungry, who have no one to look after them, no one to ease their lives."

They needed his help every bit as much as did kids in his own country. And by helping them, he'd be helping children everywhere.

Besides, I said, by reaching out to children who needed him he'd be doing a *mitzvah*—a word he understood and that brought a smile to his face—for them and for himself. It would take a load of guilt off his conscience.

And for once, he agreed with me.

"You're right," he said. "I'll even give you credit for a good idea. That's a historic first, by the way," he added.

At that point, the memory ended and was replaced by a sudden feeling, a compelling hunch. And I knew what I had to do.

Telling Alice that I had to take care of some urgent business, I set out for Harlem and the Harlem Youth Agency, known throughout the City as HYC, the place where Lenny had found a home. And where an inner voice told me I would find my man; or, at the very least, get a lead as to where he hung out.

Perhaps being around Barney is what did it, getting the hang of gumshoe thinking. Once my associations led me to the memory of the scene with Ahmed and my advice to him, the deduction was simple. Ahmed worked in the hospital, as I did, and, like me, from time to time he called on the Social Work Department to help with a patient who needed its services. He knew Sally Lombardo, had worked with her on cases, and, like me, he would have gone to her, Director of Volunteers, for help in his new quest. And since it was well known that Ahmed was one of her favorite doctors, she would have recommended the agency she liked best; the one where she had placed my brother.

It all added up, and if my unconscious had done its job and made the right links, it had done double duty. It had solved the puzzle as to where Lenny and Ahmed had met.

The agency was at the corner of 137th Street and St. Nicholas Avenue, one of the busiest intersections in Harlem. I found parking a block away and walked to the building, a stolid, eight story Depression Era structure that, in its drabness, accurately represented the mood of the period.

The front door was heavy, difficult to open, the lobby dimly lit and spare. Its floor, reflecting the color-tone of the entire building, was laid with gray tiles that looked as though they had not been successfully cleaned in years.

On the wall directly opposite the door was a Directory of tenants. There were a dozen of these, with HYC occupying two full floors.

Under the agency's name were listed those of its officers, with that of the Director, one LaToya Green, at the head of the column. Nowhere did Ahmed Aslam's name appear.

I was not surprised. If what I'd heard most recently about him was true and he'd returned to the City, he would have made sure to keep himself well hidden. Still, I found myself disappointed, as though I had been looking forward to seeing an old friend who failed to show up for our reunion.

As I stood there, scrutinizing the Directory, I heard footsteps behind me. I turned and saw a small Black man dressed in half a uniform; grey doorman-type jacket and unpressed, blue trousers.

"You are looking for someone you can't find, right?" the man asked. His name was Carl, and he was, as he explained, a combination of doorman- guard who had worked in the building for fifteen years. He had been observing me from a dark corner of the lobby.

"That's right."

"Name?"

"Ahmed. Dr. Ahmed Aslam."

"You've' hit the jackpot, my friend. Dr. Aslam is my favorite. The man is one generous human being. Do you know what he did when I was in the hospital with pneumonia? He sent me five hundred dollars. Anonymous. Just like that, just left an envelope with my name on it at the front desk. Of course, I knew who it was. No one else but Dr. Aslam would do a thing like that. He's a favorite with the kids, too. There's nothing he won't do for them and they know it. The man is a gem. You are a friend of his?"

"I am, but I haven't seen him for a while."

"He'll be here tomorrow. Comes in a couple times a week. Busy doctoring the rest of the time. Come back tomorrow. If you're an old friend, he'll be glad to see you. He's a loner, Dr. Aslam is. You won't see him hanging out with HYC people much. He probably could use an old friend."

"Thanks for the info. I'll be back. I'll see you again."

"I'll be here," Carl said. "You can bank on that."

Returning to the street I felt dizzy, light headed. When I reached my car, I half slid, half tumbled into the driver's seat.

I could not believe what had just happened. I had located Ahmed. After better than six years, I had found him. Instantly, on impulse, I looked up HYC's number on the internet, dialed it and was connected to the Director's office. I explained to her secretary that I was Leonard Strickman's brother and that I was interested in visiting the agency that had meant so much to him. And, I added, I wanted to do something to honor his memory.

The woman on the other end was enthusiastic and immediately arranged for me to meet the Director at eleven the next morning.

It was going to happen. After better than six years, after all the rumors about him, I was going to reconnect with Ahmed. But would I actually be meeting, the surgeon I worked alongside of to salvage torn limbs, to spare lives, the most skilled and dedicated physician on the service, or someone transformed, a person whose mind had been warped by messages of hate, and who now was on a very different kind of mission?

As I reflected on this question, I found myself reaffirming a long-held conviction of mine; that no matter how life impacts people, no matter what surface changes it affects, at base, and in their essence, people do not change. No matter what he'd lived through, no matter what the intervening years had brought, Ahmed would be Ahmed.

But I couldn't shake Alice's voice, which again I heard sounding the warning that she'd issued at the very start of our investigation.

"Whatever you do, keep your wits about you, Bill," she had said," You could be walking into real danger. This Ahmed doesn't know what Lenny told us, or even if he told us anything at all. But if he gets it into his head that Lenny shared what he knew with us, that could set off an alarm. In fact, right this moment your old pal could be planning something just for us; arranging to send us to a nice quiet spot in the countryside for an extended visit to your brother."

I told myself that this was Alice, forever expecting disaster, that her mind was working overtime. But I was uneasy. I couldn't rid myself of her voice.

Back home my best bet, I decided, was to call Barney, lay out the situation to him, and develop a plan. Barney would know how to handle things.

"At the 23rd we had plans up the wazoo," he had told me. "Strategies for everything from crowd control to staking out Mafia headquarters. There wasn't a perp in the City who could out-think us." Our guys had seen everything. And we had smarts," he added, "We had *sechel*."

That is just the attitude I need, I thought to myself as I reached for the phone; that and a dose of that *sechel*.

Barney was at the Hotel Pearl scouting the place, asking questions, but when he heard the anxiety in my voice, he came right over. And after hearing how I'd managed to locate Ahmed, he had a compliment for me.

"You're a natural, Doc," he said. "You've got the instincts of the best gumshoes. When we search for evidence, we start with what we know, what we've taken in without necessarily being aware of it. That's something you understand. You've been doing that kind of detective work for years, so I figured you knew a lot more about this Ahmed than you realized. And you came through for us, Doc. You've got us a lead. Your job now is to go undercover."

I turned to look at Barney. He was a couple of inches shorter than me and I found myself staring at a bald spot.

"That's way above my pay-grade, partner," I said. Snooping like that is out of my league. That's where you take over."

"Ordinarily, no problem. Going undercover is my thing. I've been them all; winos, druggies, pimps, thieves, you name it. And I've made a lot of collars that way. But in this situation, you're our man. You're the one with the perfect cover story, the grieving brother who wants to honor Lenny, contribute to the cause he cared about. What's more natural than your visiting the place that meant so much to him. You'll get a line on this outfit, find out what goes on there. And you'll see your old buddy, get a feel for who he is now, what he's doing at this kid's place. You'll get the info we need."

"Makes sense, partner" I said. "But you've got the wrong man for the job. When it comes to role-playing, I'm a total bust. My Halloween costumes never fooled anybody. The moment I walk into that place, the jig will be up; they will spot me as a phony and throw me out on my ear."

"You're no phony, Doc. You're the genuine article. Just do your thing. The two of you haven't seen each other in half-dozen years. The man will talk. He'll catch you up. Just tune in with that third ear of yours. You'll pick up what we need to know."

Chapter 3

Our reunion turned out to be a rollercoaster.

It had been six years since I laid eyes on Ahmed, but just seeing that face again, hearing that voice and the effusive way he greeted me, made me grin, lifted my spirts, triggered memories. They rushed in, recollections of the way we worked side-by-side in the E.R., of the great team we were, of the bond of friendship that grew between us.

That good feeling lasted until about halfway through my visit. Then, as I listened to Ahmed's story, heard about all that happened to him and felt the hurt, the pain, and the anger that came through in the telling—anger that was not without a wish for vengeance—I found myself beginning to wonder where the truth lay. Was it possible that Ahmed could actually have murdered my brother?

That thought should have raised fury in me, and it did, but that was later. My first response me was pain; pain and deep sadness. It ripped me open to think that way, but the idea began to inhabit my brain, to torture me

We met just outside Ahmed's office. First, though, I was obliged to field questions from the Director, LaToya Green, a veteran social work-Administrator who, after extending condolences on my loss, gently probed for any reasons, beyond honoring my brother, I might have for wanting to know about the Center.

Leonard Strickman, she explained, although a good and valuable man, had a way of ruffling more than a few feathers, and she was not looking to have more problems from another Strickman.

Reasonably satisfied that I was not a miscreant bent on some kind of troublemaking, she walked me up a flight of stairs to Ahmed's office, praising him all the way as an extraordinary man, a true gift to the children in her program.

I did not have to wait more than ten minutes for Ahmed to appear. But that was long enough for me to feel rising anxiety at not knowing who was about to walk through his door.

As I was thinking about this and trying to calm myself, he emerged. On each side of him were two burly men, both clearly Arabs, who had the wary and menacing look of bodyguards.

When he spotted me, Ahmed stopped in mid-step and let out a cry, "Siggie"—this was the nickname, short for Sigmund, with which Ahmed had branded me from the first day we met. Then he broke from his companions, came rushing forward, and, as I rose, embraced me with an all-enveloping bear hug. Then he stepped back and looked me over.

"My God, is it really you? I can't believe it. It's been how long, half a dozen years? At least that. It's amazing. You look exactly the same, the same Siggie the shrink. How the hell are you, man?"

"Not too bad for an old Freudian. And you?"

"I'm okay. More than okay. I'm good." He waved an arm in a vaguely circular motion.

"Being here, working with these kids, it keeps me young."

"That's great."

Ahmed turned toward the men who came out with him.

"Siggie, I want you to meet my two right hands, Abdul and Moham-med. They work with me and do all they can to keep my head on straight. "Gentlemen, this is Dr. William Strickman, an old friend. We did a stint together in the ER a hundred years ago. We sewed up a lot of limbs that year, didn't we, Siggie?"

"Set a hospital record as I remember."

"We were quite a team, Siggie and me. I kept telling him that he missed his calling. This man has good hands and a way with a scalpel. He would have made a great surgeon but he wouldn't listen. He insisted on going the shrink route, even though the poor guy knew nothing about psychology and less about dreams. I had to teach him everything."

Ahmed was referring to a matter he loved to tease me about. When we met I hadn't yet begun my psychiatric training, and, as Ahmed said, I was pretty ignorant about psychological matters. And about dreams I knew nothing. Ahmed, on the other hand, knew a great deal.

Before he made the switch to pre-med, he was a psychology major and well read in that field. His father, a psychiatrist, the first in Lebanon to establish a study group on Freud's writings, was his tutor. In his senior year at college, father and son collaborated on a paper about dreams and their formation that was published in a psychology journal.

Ahmed liked nothing better than to challenge me to interpret his dreams. Even while we were setting a broken leg or stitching up a laceration, he might suddenly recite a dream and demand an interpretation. He liked to put me on the spot, and to get back at him I would come up with some raunchy stuff, interpreting whatever he told me as reflecting his perverse wishes, including bestiality and cannibalism. He would roar with laughter and insist that my interpretations were nothing but projections of my dark and twisted nature.

"Someday, when you are in your own analysis, you'll see that I was right, Siggie," he would say. "Your nice guy pose is just a mask. You are as horny and perverted as the rest of us. And when you've become a brilliant psychoanalyst and master dream interpreter, don't forget who your first teacher was."

"How could I forget," I'd reply. "It will take me a good decade to unlearn all the psycho-babble you've stuffed into my head."

That was the easy part. We loved to tease one another and to experience the camaraderie that lay just beneath our jousting.

More difficult were our arguments. Almost always they centered on the issue that preoccupied him; the unsolvable struggle between Israel and the Palestinians. A brilliant debater, he marshaled his arguments so skillfully that he could—and did—vanquish any opponent who took him on.

Ahmed always claimed that his fight was with the Israeli government, that he had nothing against Jewish people. And for the most part I believed him. But I had come to question if that were possible. Could a man hate Israel, the homeland of the Jews, and not hate the people who live there? In his debates with the staff, was Ahmed's go-for-the-throat attitude toward his Jewish doctor adversaries solely his debating style? Or did it reveal a deep, underlying animus toward Jews? I wondered if it was this uncertainty, my doubt about his true feelings, that was behind my willingness to give up the search for him.

Ahmed motioned for me to come into his office. He took his place behind a large unadorned desk and I sat alongside in the visitor's chair. As he settled himself, I took a close look at him. He appeared a good deal older, with a certain weightiness—or was it some unspoken sadness—about him. But when he described his work at the Center, there was much of the old spirit, the enthusiasm for what he was doing, that I had found so appealing.

As we talked, I recalled more of our year together and how much I'd admired his skills and appreciated all that he taught me. It was he who made sure that I knew how, in dealing with severely injured patients, to take the steps needed to preserve life.

His co-workers, seeing that Ahmed was caught up with his visitor, excused themselves and with what seemed like military precision, marched off.

"Good men," Ahmed declared, watching them go. "Disciplined people. Hard working. Mohammed is Abdul's uncle. The kids call him Uncle M. He's devoted to the job, identifies with these kids, and strives to give them a chance in life. Also devoted to our cause."

I did not have to ask what that was: a free State of their own for the Palestinians, along with recognition by, and citizenship in, the world community. And also, I thought to myself, the quick and thorough demolition of the State of Israel.

We had been talking for some time, and Ahmed had said nothing about Lenny. That seemed odd to me, and suspicious. I asked if he had heard about my brother.

"I heard this morning, Siggie," he said. "I'm sorry for your loss."

The words were there, and I realized that Ahmed was trying to reach out to me. But the flatness in his voice betrayed his true feelings. I suspected that Ahmed was not sorry that Lenny was gone. I understood this, but I resented that my old friend could not bring himself to utter even a few words in recognition of Lenny's contribution to the Center.

Ahmed sensed my feelings.

"Leonard was a difficult man, Siggie," he said. "You must know that."

I said nothing.

"What he tried to do undermined our program," Ahmed went on, "No offense, Siggie, but the man was impossible. Actually, I've never known anyone like him. Leonard Strickman must have been the most stubborn man in the universe. Once he'd made his mind up about something, a bulldozer couldn't budge him. A dozen people could show him he was wrong. It made no difference. Leonard Strickman knew better."

Ahmed's tone grew sharper. "I tell you, Siggie, your brother could get to me like no one else. There were times when I just wanted to throttle him, and in my dreams I came damn close to doing just that."

"But you didn't. Was that because Lenny looked so much like me?"

Ahmed laughed and gave me a mock punch.

"As usual, Siggie, your interpretation is way off. If that were the case, I'd have done the job one, two, three. I missed my chance, though, so I guess I'll have to contend with you again. But I warn you, Siggie, I'm tougher these days."

"We'll see about that," I retorted.

I looked closely at him. Anger still clouded his face. I could see how it could have taken him over, driven him to kill.

Ahmed then went on to describe the big trouble my brother had caused. According to him, Lenny started lecturing his mentee, a disturbed twelve-year-old boy, about Jewish history.

"Gave him the full treatment," Ahmed said. "The Nazis, the Holocaust, the camps, and, of course, the fight against the bad guys, the Arabs, who didn't want the Jews to have their own home. The boy takes it all in and starts talking to the other kids. Word gets around that the Arabs are inhuman brutes just like the Nazis.

"It was intolerable, Siggie, the way Lenny maligned our people. He created a furor here. There was talk about doing your brother in, and, frankly, I wasn't surprised."

Ahmed said nothing about the broadcast and his attack on Lenny, nothing about my brother's threat to expose him and his crew for some wrong doing. Nothing at all of substance about Lenny's death. Clearly he was avoiding the subject.

It struck me then that what I was hearing about my brother could not be true. Ahmed's description of him was not the Lenny I knew. My brother was an enthusiastic teacher, cared deeply about the Jewish people and all they had suffered. And was surely pro-Israel, but he was no proselytizer. He hated that kind of thing and was highly critical of people whose religious biases distorted the facts of history. No, this was not my brother. It was the way Ahmed and his cronies needed to see him.

But I said nothing. I didn't want to start a fight. I was there to learn, to understand who Ahmed was, who he had become; to discover if the man I knew and loved was still there.

I changed the subject.

"I am sorry I didn't keep up with you, Ahmed," I said. "I meant to, but somehow something always came up to distract me."

"I know what you mean, Siggie. It was the same with me. We both dropped the ball."

"Actually, I was going to call you at one point—this was almost, but not quite, true— "but I was told that you had left the country."

"For four years. Four long years," he replied. "My father died suddenly and I needed to go. It took me a long time to get back and pick up my life. They say a man doesn't come into his own until his father dies. For me it was the reverse. When I lost him, I went into a nose dive. He was my anchor and support. I had no idea how much I relied on him. For a few years I just wandered around the region, practically the whole Middle East; Pakistan, Yemen, parts of Afghanistan, you name it. And I got a real feel for what my people have been going through. Many work seven days a week and bring home a couple of dollars a day, barely enough to survive. And their lands are being exploited by foreign companies who are supported by their oil-hungry governments. It made me sick to see it, Siggie. This is genocide."

Ahmed went on to describe how helpless he felt at that time, how lost. A boat adrift, rudderless..

"Between losing my father and taking in the wretchedness all around me, I was a mental case, Siggie. I needed you then but without benefit of your couch I did my own analyzing and I realized the only thing that would make a difference would be to take action, to be part of the solution."

At that point he said he sought out and joined an activist group.

"People who work for change, who don't merely sit on the sidelines," was the way he put it.

Exactly what kind of group this was, Ahamed didn't say. Deliberately did not say. But there was no need to. In Ahmed's part of the world an activist group meant only one thing. Islamic militants bent on carrying out Jihad, the total destruction of the enemies of Allah.

As Ahmed continued to describe his life abroad, his efforts to support his fellow Arabs, do whatever he could for them, and his ultimate decision to return to New York, pick up his old life, and organize the Arab community, I found my mind drifting. I wondered how I would have behaved if I were in Ahmed's shoes, drawn to the Jihad cause with its teachings about the tyranny of Western Nations,, their inhumanity and greed. If I had joined a militant group, would my mind have been drastically altered, my brain fundamentally changed? Would I have been ready to eliminate anyone who stood in my way, who blocked my need to strike a blow for justice, for the rights of my people?

Was this Ahmed's journey, the road my old friend had taken? Increasingly I was beginning to think so, to accept Alice's view. For her the radio transcript said it all; Ahmed had killed my brother to eliminate the danger of his being exposed and his mission—whatever it was—destroyed.

Was I now agreeing with my wife, seeing things her way because the evidence was supporting her argument, or was it to push away the thought that had crept into my mind as I listened to Ahmed; the idea that despite the hurt and pain that he suffered, Ahmed was not a killer, that it wasn't in him to have murdered my brother. Also the confusing thought that had also invaded my consciousness; that, in fact, no one had killed Lenny; that he had taken his own life because he could no longer live with the pain of living. And I had done nothing to prevent this, nothing to help him live.

I focused again on Ahmed, reminding myself that I needed to listen to him as I had learned to listen over the years; to the tones and overtones of speech, its pace and rhythm, to the pauses and inflections, to what is said and what is unsaid.

I turned the conversation to Ahmed's father.

"What happened to your Dad, Ahmed?" I asked.

For a moment he did not reply. He just looked at me, seeming to appraise me, trying, perhaps, to assess just how I would take what he was about to say.

"He was killed by the Israelis," he finally said. Visiting cousins in a Palestinian village. There was a raid. The Israeli army was looking for terrorists who had fired rockets across the border. They targeted a house where they thought these men were hiding. Destroyed it with a missile. Only problem was the terrorists weren't there. They never had been. A dozen civilians were killed, including my dad. And why? Because a rocket from Gaza had killed an Israeli woman. Twelve to one. How is that for justice?

"The Israelis claimed it was a mistake, acknowledged they hit the wrong house. No apology, just that statement. Collateral damage. The price Palestinians have to pay for daring to strike back. And what do a dozen dead Arabs matter anyway? Arabs are scum, everyone knows that."

I said nothing. I could feel Ahmed's pain, understand his bitterness. But I also found myself bristling at his one-sided characterization of the Israelis. This was not the time to speak, though. It was a time to listen.

"What hurt most, Siggie, was that my father was a man of peace. He renounced violence as totally useless, as begetting nothing but more violence. I tried to show him that there are times when it is necessary, the only answer to brute aggression. But for him the use of force was always self-defeating. He believed that progress can only be made through talk, negotiations, and reason. He joined peace groups and had good friendships with Israeli colleagues. It didn't matter. Nothing mattered. They killed him anyway."

I reached out and touched my old friend's arm. "I am terribly sorry, Ahmed."

He shrugged. "It woke me up, Siggie. I realized for the first time what the Israelis have become. They've hardened into brutes, just like the Germans. They kill with ease, and rationalize their brutality as necessary, as purely self-protective. That was how the Nazis explained their sadism. It's sad, Siggie, but the Israelis have become more like them than they know. It's a tragedy, not only for us, the victims, but for them as well. They have lost their humanity."

"It's been lost on both sides," I said. "and there's no end in sight."

"The end will come when the Israelis realize that they are playing a losing game," he replied. "They have to be made to see that."

I sensed where this now was heading and I did not want to go there. Years ago, when we worked together, that statement would have roused me to take Ahmed on and we would have launched one of our epic battles. Now I held back. I felt Ahmed's grief. The wound was still fresh, still raw. It had changed him. No doubt about that. He was tougher, more resolute, more determined to take action that would make a difference. But in what way? How far was Ahmed prepared to go, or had he already gone, to prove that there are times when violence is necessary, when it is the only way.

So I did not take him on. Instead I asked about Marco and how he was doing. If I was to take Lenny's place and be his mentor, I would need to know as much as possible about him.

"He was coming along," Ahmed replied, "making real headway. But when we objected to Lenny's propaganda, he got confused. He withdrew and became silent again. He doesn't know about your brother yet. We haven't told him. Frankly we're worried. He's liable to take Lenny's death as another abandonment."

"Probably inevitable with a child like that. And the last thing he needs is another loss. Can the mother be helpful?" Ahmed now seemed to brighten.

"Thank God for her, Siggie. This woman is a gem. She understands what this loss means to the boy and she's totally supportive. I've gotten to know her, Siggie. We've gotten close. Listen, Sig, keep this under your hat. LaToya might not be too happy to hear this from anyone. We've been seeing one another, Laura and I. Socially, I mean."

"I know what you mean, Ahmed."

"She's Jewish, Sig. This is a first for me. I never thought I'd be involved with a Jewish woman. No offense, Siggie, you understand what I am saying?"

I nodded. "I get it. You've finally seen the light. It's taken a long time to get it through that thick skull of yours that Jewish women are the best. Get yourself a good one and she'll be loyal, even to an infidel like you."

"Spoken like a true chauvinist."

"Actually, a realist, my friend. Your Arab stubbornness has blinded you. You've been unable to see the obvious. But I congratulate you. You are starting to emerge from the Dark Ages."

"My vision was always clear. I was waiting for the right one to appear. And she has. Laura is a wonder."

"She'd have to be to deal with a dinosaur like you. Do you remember when you wouldn't date at all? You made every excuse to cover it up. Told us that you dated only Muslims, then only those who read the Qur'an and prayed umpteen times a day. The truth is, you were afraid of women, a classic case of incest anxiety. You loved your mother too much, Ahmed.

You talked about needing a Muslim woman, but, unconsciously, they, too, were taboo; too close to mama."

"Always with the two-bit interpretations, Siggie. It's a compulsion. Unfortunately, I listened to you and now see where I am? With an anti-mother, a Jewish lady. Talk about taboos. I'm in real trouble. When my people find out about this, they are liable to murder me."

"Not to worry. We Jews will protect you. We'll take you in. I know a Rabbi who specializes in converting Muslims." I felt like adding the word, radicals, but kept my mouth shut.

"Seriously Siggie," Ahmed said, "I've found a jewel. This is someone who really gets me. She is not only smart, she's the most open-minded person I know. She's not one of those Jews who automatically defends Israel. She's spent time in the Territories and she understands what my people have been through. She's seen the suffering so she can understand my feelings. She gets me and she shares my views."

"Well that's good," I replied. "I don't imagine things would go well if she shared mine."

Ahmed laughed. "You I can tolerate," he said, "but I don't go to bed with you."

"Would it be possible for me to talk with your friend?" I asked. "I'd like to know her thoughts about my brother."

I knew it was important to talk with Laura as the mother of the child Lenny mentored. She could give me an objective view of what truly happened at the Center and might have insights into Ahmed—the new Ahmed—that could prove valuable. How committed was he, for instance, to the Jihad mission and how determined to avenge his father's death? Also, she might have heard something about Ahmed's intentions with regard to my brother; some inside information that only someone close to Ahmed would know. Whether she would talk about him, however, was another matter. It would take time to get to know her and to win her confidence. Frankly, I didn't know if I was up for the job, but if she could give us what we needed, it was worth a shot.

"I don't see why not, but don't expect kudos for your brother," Ahmed said, "Laura had very mixed feelings about him."

"I imagine you exerted a strong influence on her' is what I wanted to say, but I kept my mouth shut.

"I get it," I replied. "But I'd still like to hear what the lady has to say."

Ahmed looked at his watch.

"Okay. You might even be able to talk with her today. She's gotten involved with the Center as a volunteer working with kids with learning problems. She works in a room off the library. I'll call down and see if she's still here."

Ahmed returned to his office, made a quick call. Then he was back.

"The librarian said she just left. She's probably on her way down to the lobby. If you hurry you might catch her."

"Thanks. I'll try."

Ahmed came forward and hugged me again.

"Great to see you, Siggie. Wonderful surprise. Don't keep yourself a stranger."

"I won't. Actually, we need to talk. I'm thinking of volunteering myself, doing what I can to carry on Lenny's work."

For a moment Ahmed did not reply. He looked away.

"We'll talk," he finally said, "We'll have to look into that."

His message was clear. I wasn't welcome. But I let it pass. This wasn't the time to get into that. Instead, I told Ahmed how good it was to see him, said I'd be in touch, and, giving him a final wave, headed for the door.

It was quite some time since I'd seen Ahmed, and although in the months after he disappeared I thought of him often, he was not as much on my mind in recent years. But now, leaving, I experienced a surprising feeling of emptiness, a reluctance to say goodbye.

Outside Ahmed's office, I noticed the two men he had introduced me to, Mohammed and Abdul, standing in the corridor. They seemed to be keeping an eye on the entranceway to his office, waiting, or watching for something to happen.

As soon as I emerged and started for the elevators, I heard my name called. I turned, "Doctor Strickman," Abdul had moved quickly and was almost on top of me. Mohammed was a step behind.

"Do you have a moment, Doctor," Abdul was saying. "there is something we need to discuss with you."

I looked at him. He seemed agitated, "What is that?"

Mohammed stepped forward. He now was their spokesman.

"It's about your brother. Did Dr. Aslam tell you about what happened here, about the disruption he caused?

"Dr. Aslam did tell me about that. Mrs. Green did, too. Is that what you wanted to discuss?"

"And did he tell you about the problem with your being here, the danger in that?"

"I'm afraid I'm not following you."

"Then I'll speak more plainly, Doctor. Your brother wreaked havoc here. Our Muslim colleagues are enraged that he was allowed to work here. And if they find out that another Strickman has replaced him, there will be a riot. Even mayhem. You will be in danger and so will Dr. Aslam."

I heard what this man was saying but I was totally confused. Where was this coming from? I looked at Mohammed. His face was flushed with anger.

"I am not sure why you are telling me this now," I said. "I came here to visit the Center and to see my old friend, Dr. Aslam."

"I am telling you in case you had any thoughts of spending time here. That would be extremely unwise."

"I hear what you are saying and I will take this up with Dr. Aslam," I replied

Fury within me was building. These geeks were threatening me, telling me that because I was Lenny's brother—the brother who did so much for the Center and was totally devoted to the children—I'd better not show my face around here, and if I did, there would be big trouble.

I looked at these two bigots and I had the strongest urge to punch them out. They reminded me of the Irish toughs who used to follow us Jewish kids from school, corner us on a deserted street, pummel us, and order us to hand over what money we had, all the while screaming in our faces, "You people killed our Christ."

I pushed past the two of them and headed for the elevators. I could feel their eyes on me, their hostile stares following me. When I reached the elevator bank, I didn't give way to my impulse to turn around and give them the finger. I didn't want to create more trouble, which I feared would end up causing problems for Ahmed, so I just waited until an elevator came, the doors opened, and I could make my escape.

When I reached the lobby, I spotted a guard; not my friend, Carl, this time, but someone dressed similarly who was seated on a folding chair near the rear wall.

"Did a lady just come down from upstairs?" I asked, glancing at him and turning back to search the lobby again.

For some seconds he did not reply. He looked at me and said nothing, the unspoken question, 'and just who is asking,' spelled out on his face.

"I'm from the Center," I added quickly. "I need to speak to the lady who just came down." The guard barely stirred but pointed toward the front door. "Just left. Made a right out the door."

"Thanks."

"I watch these things," the guard added, "in case they're up to no good. I watch whether they go right or left. It's something extra I do."

"Good idea," I threw back as I ran for the door. "Good thinking."

Out on the street, I made a right turn and scanned the block ahead. It was crowded with shoppers and casual strollers. I could see no lone woman. Half running, half walking, I made my way through the crowd, continuing to look as far ahead as I could.

I was about a block away when I spotted a woman waiting at a bus stop with perhaps a half dozen others. She had her back to me and was at the end of the line. There was no bus in sight.

I stopped running, walked to within a few feet of her, and realized I did not know her last name. Ahmed had referred to her either as Laura or Marco's mother. I felt like a damn fool. I had run like a madman to catch up with someone who I had never met and whose name I did not know. I stood there like a school boy at a seventh-grade mixer, paralyzed in front of a pretty girl I wanted to meet.

"Excuse me," I finally managed to get out. "Marco's mother?"

The woman turned, saw an out of breath stranger accosting her. Her face registered fright.

"Yes?"

"Please don't be alarmed. There is nothing wrong. Marco is fine. I'm Bill Strickman, Leonard Strickman's brother. Do you have a few minutes? Dr. Aslam suggested that I talk with you. I have a few questions about my brother."

Laura Holtzman looked at me, searched my face.

"You are Leonard's brother?"

I nodded. She was silent, continued to look me over. Then her voice softened seemed to reach out to me.

"I am sorry for your loss," she said.

"Thank you. I appreciate that. It was all so sudden, it's hard to believe."

She nodded. "We all felt that way. Seemed like Lenny was a fixture just part of the Center.

"Working with the children meant so much to him," I said. "And he was especially fond of mentoring your son."

She nodded, smiled at me. "I know. How can I help?"

"I want to know more about my brother's work. I understand something about what he did, but not in any detail. I'd like to know how he actually mentored the children. I'm planning to give the Center a gift in his name and I want to be well enough informed so as to make it a meaningful contribution."

"That's very thoughtful of you."

Laura sounded sincere, appreciative, but there was something a bit hesitant, a bit noncommittal that came through in her tone.

"I'm glad to share what I know," she added, "but what you have in mind will take more than a few minutes, more time than I have now. Perhaps we can arrange an appointment."

"Thank you, that is very kind of you. When would it be convenient?"

"You say that Dr. Aslam suggested we speak?"

"Yes, he did. He is an old friend. We worked together at a hospital for some time."

"I see. Well, he's quite a man, your old friend."

"That I know. A remarkable person."

A bus had pulled up and people were boarding.

"I have to run now, Dr. Strickman. I'll be at the

Center again tomorrow. Can you come by at one o'clock?"

"Absolutely. And thank you."

She got on, turned and waved.

"Until tomorrow."

I stood for a moment watching the bus depart. And I found myself feeling envious of Ahmed. She was quite lovely this girlfriend of his; attractive with a certain gentleness and kindness that came through in her voice. I could see why Ahmed was drawn to her. And, obviously, she was equally taken with him. No surprise there. Ahmed Aslam was one of the most impressive people I've known.

But how much did she really know about him, I wondered; about his beliefs and who he'd become. How much had he revealed to her? Had he told her his story, about how he'd felt a need to join a militant group and to embrace Jihad?

And did Laura share his views? If so, was she in on Lenny's death? She certainly knew him well and could supply Ahmed with some useful information about his habits and whereabouts. No question, this young lady was a person of interest, as Barney would put it. She might even hold the key to what happened to my brother. I was looking forward to tomorrow.

My car was parked just a block from the Center. As I approached it, I noticed something on the windshield. From a distance it looked like a ticket and I cursed myself for being too stingy to put enough money in the meter.

As I got closer, though, and was able to slip the cardboard object out from under a wiper blade, I saw that it wasn't a ticket.

It was a photo of the entrance to the HYC building, and covering the door in red crayon was a large X. The message was clear. Stay away. You are not welcome here. And if, for any reason that message did not come through clearly enough, it was punctuated by a slashed rear tire, a concrete statement of how effectively the sender could wield a knife.

When I got home, I called Barney and his response was pure Barney.

"We will be there tomorrow, and the next day, and the day after that," he said. "They'll soon find out where their threats get them. We'll be on their tails until the only photos they can take will be of San Quentin."

"When you say, 'we'." I put in, "I assume you are using the royal 'we.' You actually mean yourself, don't you?"

"No, the two of us, you and me. You working the inside, me out-side, as your eyes and ears. That's the 23rd's double team approach. Reserved for the elite investigative unit. An inside man, and outside, his living antenna."

"And when do we switch places?" I asked.

"When a team is working well, we stick with it. No need to change."

So that was it. No use arguing with Barney, that I had learned early on. We were stuck together, he and I. I couldn't complain. I had chosen him, 50-inch waist and all. Now I had to live with my new identity; inside man on the Barney version of the 23rd's elite investigative unit. So be it. Something to tell my grandchildren about. If I survived.

Chapter 4

Ahmed Aslam sat alone in his office. He was glad to be alone, to reflect, to think about the unexpected visit from Siggie and the situation, the thorny situation, it created.

He had sent Mohammed and Abdul to look for office space to use as their team's headquarters and also to set up a classroom, a place to teach religion to the children from the Center. It was especially important to teach them about the Muslim religion and how it is misunderstood and distorted by its enemies in the U.S.

It was a relief now to have some time to himself, not to have to deal with Mohammed and Abdul's questions about what plans he was making for their team, why he had done this and not that, why, particularly, he had not acted sooner, more decisively, on the Lenny situation.

And now, of course, they would be at him about Siggie's visit. They would want to know why he hadn't avoided the whole problem, claimed he was too busy or had one of them say he was unavailable. They would fault him for being welcoming to another Strickman when the brother had caused so much trouble. And among themselves they would question his judgment, his commitment to them and to what they were here to accomplish.

He hated that kind of pressure and the steady stream of criticism that accompanied it. And he noticed that Mohammed and Abdul had started talking to each other and not to him. It was clear that they now questioned his ability as a leader. He would wager, in fact, that they had taken it on themselves to speak to Siggie on his way out, to tell him, in essence, not to come back, that his presence would only cause trouble.

Of course, they were right, but the situation was complex. If Siggie became suspicious, started poking around, asking questions, there could be big trouble. He had to be handled carefully, tactfully. A quick move to get rid of him could backfire, make him more suspicious.

He had to be careful, too, of his own feelings about Siggie; couldn't let his friendship cloud his judgment. That was a problem in himself that he was aware of and so was Mohammed. Since their dissatisfaction with his handling of the Lenny problem—they wanted him to get rid of the troublesome Jew immediately—Mohammed and Abdul had been watching him. He knew they would act fast, take the reins themselves if he showed any signs of indecisiveness.

At times like this he found it helpful to write to his father. The fact that his father was no longer living, that he hadn't had an actual father for many years, did not matter. His father was with him at all times, always a source of good advice, of sound judgment, of wisdom derived from long experience working with people in distress.

He hoped his father would provide guidance in this situation, show him a path forward. He was confused and made anxious by the tense atmosphere at the Center and the criticism, spoken and unspoken, of him for not being tough enough, bold enough, for not serving the interests of the Muslim staff and the special mission of his own team.

And he realized he would be in danger himself if he did not handle this Siggie problem properly. Any suggestion that he was being hesitant, reluctant to act, any hint that he was not wholly on their side, any question of his loyalty, and the two of them, Mohammed and Abdul, would turn on him. That he knew.

Ahmed's style in writing to his father was always informal, colloquial, a manner half way between sharing thoughts with an old friend and freely associating as a patient on his father's couch.

"I was surprised by Siggie showing up Dad," he began. "I shouldn't have been. He's a smart guy, a persistent guy, and I should have known that at some point he'd find me. I should have planned for it, done a better job of preparing in case it happened; I underestimated the danger.

But I deceived myself into believing that after six years of looking for me, he'd call it quits. Or, if he started looking again because of Lenny's death, he'd come up as empty handed as he had before. And I was influenced by Lenny saying that he mentioned nothing about me to Siggie. Not that we worked in the same place, not even that he knew me. At first that puzzled me. I couldn't figure out what that was about. But once I got a line on Lenny Strickman and realized that we were going to go head to head; that this was going to be warfare and that he knew it, too, I understood. Lenny didn't want Siggie to be torn between us, to have to take sides. He was protective of his brother in that way. He didn't want to add to Siggie's burdens.

But there was something else, too. Lenny didn't want to confront the fact that Siggie and I got along, that we were long-time friends. He didn't want that to influence him, to cause him to question himself and his attitude toward me. He was a hard ass, Lenny was. And he would not consider the possibility that if Siggie got along with me, maybe I wasn't the horror, the Jew hater he was convinced I was. Or that maybe something I said was actually valid. He wanted to see me, my team, and all the Muslims here as blindly hostile to him, to his work with the kid, Marco, and to Jewish people in and outside of Israel.

He was a fierce guy, Lenny was, and most of the time fiercely wrong. But he never could see that. Facts didn't matter to him, history didn't matter. Only what Lenny Strickman knew to be true, mattered. As you used to say about some thick-skulled people you knew, they forgot to get on line when the Lord was handing out the genes for self-reflection.

But that is neither here nor there, Dad. Siggie showed up and that's a threat, a big one for us and for me personally. If he picks up info about our operation and discovers what Lenny knew, he'll figure out what happened. We'll need to send him packing before he can do that.

Not that some part of me isn't glad to see him. I've missed the guy. He reminds me of some of the Jewish friends you had; straightforward, what you see is what you get.

But Siggie and Lenny are from the same family and Siggie can be as obstinate and closed minded about Israel as his brother. When we fought at the hospital, I would remind him that it's not Kosher to try to write his own version of history just because he doesn't like the original. That's what Lenny would do. Siggie has taken lessons from the master.

But Siggie is not Lenny. He is trained as a shrink. He knows how to listen. It takes some doing, but I can get through to him. He's come to understand a lot of what I've told him about our people, what we've been through, what it's like trying to exist, to build a life when an enormous weight is pressing down on you, stifling you, taking the air out of your lungs. And you have no vitality, no spirit left.

I've wanted him to understand, still want him to understand, the way you wanted some of your Israeli colleagues to understand what life in the Territories is like.

For some reason it still is important to me that Siggie understand about my life and the decision I've made. I tried to explain that to him. He listened, but I don't know if he got it. He's American, he's lived in a cocoon, he's never known brutality, violence. I don't know if he can put himself in my shoes, really understand my need after years of sitting on the sidelines and watching our people suffer, to raise a fist against that brutality, that crushing oppression.

I didn't write to him when I made the decision to make the change, to stop living on the periphery. I didn't think that he would understand and that we'd end up enemies.

But then yesterday I found myself hoping that he would get it, that he could imagine himself into my life; that for a few minutes, he could get into my head.

Why that is so important to me I really don't know. Perhaps he stands in for you. The two of you are very different, but in some ways, he reminds me of you. Maybe it's because both of you are shrinks and you chose a profession in which you listen and try to understand other people's lives, other worlds and dreams. And the fact that he's into dreams reminds me of you. You taught me about dreams, how they carry our wishes into the daylight. Siggie's also fascinated by dreams. He shares our interest. When he was starting out, I taught him what you taught me. He's not you, Dad. You're still the Master. But in his own way he's carrying on your legacy. And somehow that's important to me. And there is something else about him that's like you. He's one of the few people I've known who truly cares about me. But he's a problem, Dad. Make no mistake about that. He wants to spend time here, to carry on his brother's work. And he wants me to speak to LaToya for him.

He couldn't have come up with anything that's more likely to do us both in. I'm serious, Dad. If he tries to join our team, the two of them, Mohammed and Abdul, are going to put unbelievable pressure on me to get rid of him. And you know what that means. Eliminate him. Take no chances that he's picked up something that could hurt us. And if I don't do that fast, I'll be next in line. They are already watching every move I make, waiting for a misstep. These two don't understand that if you act precipitously, make an abrupt move, you immediately become suspicious.

All eyes are on you. You are under constant scrutiny and you are boxed in. You can't function, can't operate with any degree of freedom.

I'm going to have to convince our people that Siggie will have to be with us for a while. That's the safest course for the moment. In time we'll find a way to move him out, but for now this is the only way to avoid suspicion.

It's going to be a hard sell, though, Dad. Abdul and Mohammed are already talking about him being an informer for the police, that he's a danger, and that I need to pack him off quickly, send him on a long visit to his brother. And given their current suspicions about me, they are liable to make getting rid of Siggie a test of my loyalty. They'll remind me of my pledge to serve the Cause no matter what the cost.

And it's true that I took that pledge, Dad, because I believed that it was the right thing to do. I know that you would never have done that. I thought of what you'd say, that the true aim of these people is to kill Jews, kill all infidels. I don't see it that way, don't see wanton killing as their motivation. But maybe in the end you'll turn out to be right, I don't know. What I do know is that it's hard, truly hard, for me to carry out that pledge. I've not succeeded in every assignment I've had, but I'm committed to our goals and I've done some things I could never have imagined doing. And I have to keep on doing them. If I don't, my two buddies will take out Siggie and put a target on my back as well.

This is unfamiliar territory for me, Dad, a long way from what I'm used to. It's a lot easier to stand at an operating table, repair wounds, work to save a life. But there are times when priorities shift, goals become bigger, and you have to be concerned with a peoples' survival. I know that you worked toward the same goal, worked for peace, but perhaps you learned that in our situation peace can't happen without a fight, without our willingness to spill blood. That's the only language the Israelis and their friends understand. Anyway, that's my take on things. I hope I'm right. Either way, I need you by my side; need your voice, your steady hand.

"One wrong move with Siggie and we're finished. I'm finished. My pals here will break up our team, put an end to our mission and an even quicker end to my tenure on this earth.

"But I know you're there for me. You always were and you always will be. Just give me the strength to see things clearly and to do the right thing.

"I'll write you again soon, Dad, I'm always thinking of you. Rest easy."

Chapter 5

Our plan was to meet after we'd carried out our missions, me to reconnect with Ahmed, Barney to scout out the Pearl Hotel, learn what he could about my brother's visits there and who had access to his room in the hours before his death.

I was anxious to see Barney, report on my meeting with Ahmed, and based on what he told about his so-called activism, get Barney's take on the question that now burned in my head, had begun to torment me. Could it be that his conversion and the indoctrination he received have led him to act against his own nature, his deepest instincts, and to take a human life? What we knew so far pointed that way, but to me the facts also pointed in another direction; toward the unfathomable.

Not that I expected Barney to have the answer. But he'd been around a lot of violence in his time, a lot of killing. And he'd seen his share of folks with bad blood toward one another. He had a sense of the kinds of things that drove people over the edge, caused them to pull triggers or to throttle an enemy.

I also wanted to tell him about Laura and get his thoughts on another puzzle; one that I'd been ruminating on since I met her.

What could have led a person like her, an intelligent, thoughtful, seemingly kind hearted woman to involve herself with someone who endorsed hatred, the slaughter of innocent people, and the destruction of the Jewish homeland.

And I was hoping Barney would help me work out a strategy for my meeting with her, one that had a chance of heading off a highly likely scenario; my putting both feet in my mouth, either together or one at a time. I'd been known to do it both ways.

When Barney arrived, though, he was in no condition to talk about anything.

"Look at me, Doc," he began as he came in breathing hard, sweat making his face glisten. "Do I look yellow?" he asked, "my face definitely yellowish?"

"Not that I can see."

"Well it should be. I've got enough egg on my face for a three-egg omelet."

"What are you talking about?"

"Hutzpah, your partner's specialty. When I heard your story, I told myself Steiner might be wrong, that this time he might have been too quick on the trigger. Mind you, this is me, the old beat cop second guessing the Chief of Detectives who's been on the job for thirty-five years. That's the kind of hutzpah that can get you a lot of egg on your face."

"Are you telling me that Steiner was right after all?"

"Looks like that. What we have so far points that way. I still have questions I want answered, but at the moment it looks like Steiner got the picture right away."

At that point, looking exhausted, Barney squeezed himself into an armchair. For a minute he sat in silence, looking like a beached porpoise. Then he continued.

"I got hold of both hotel clerks," he said, "the fellow who starts at noon and the night clerk. Both told me the same thing. Your brother was a regular. Showed up on an average of once a month, mostly on weekends, stayed a night or two, and signed out. Always had the hookers come up to his room. Mostly the same ones; hustlers who work the area and are well known to the hotel staff. They'd stay a couple of hours and leave. Apparently, Lenny paid well. There was never any trouble."

"So what the detective told me was correct. My brother lived his life hiding his big secret."

Barney nodded. "Probably born gay and couldn't face it. I've seen quite a few like that. Sad people. They hide out their whole lives. Can't accept who they are. A night or two at a place like this is their only outlet. It seems awful, pretty sordid, but it's what they can manage, so who are we to judge?"

Barney seemed to be thinking out loud, weighing what he knew so far and deciding how to report what he had learned.

"I quizzed both clerks as to anyone who'd visited your brother close to the time they found his body. The only one they knew of was the Hooker. Of course someone else could have gotten upstairs, slipped by and taken the stairs without being seen, but the kid is the only one for sure. This guy's been working the area for a couple of years. He pays off the clerks to look the other way. I got a description and called some buddies of mine in the neighborhood. They knew the kid, knew right away who I meant. He's got a long rap sheet. Been pinched a number of times for prostitution, also petty larceny, and once for breaking and entering. My friend, Paul, who's been a detective in the precinct forever— he's ready to call it quits and come fishing with me—did me favor and picked the kid up. Didn't book him. Just scared the crap out of him and brought him over to the hotel."

"And?"

"And nothing. Zip. *Bupkis.* I figured if this was a homicide, the person we want to speak to first is the one who was alone with your brother in the hours before he died. Things can get rough in these situations. It's possible that the kid got riled up for some reason, put his hands on Lenny, started to choke him, and couldn't stop. It happens. Or maybe he smothers him with a pillow, then strings him up. Something like that could have happened and the cops just missed it because they were thinking suicide. That's what they had in their heads and they couldn't think of anything else.

Anyhow, I grilled the kid personally. I really went after him. I told him we knew he did it, that we had evidence. I pressured him to confess. It didn't work and in the end I believed his story I think he was being straight. There was no fight, no argument, just the usual encounter; a blow job, jerking each other off, that kind of thing. They were together for maybe an hour, tops. Seems that your brother was a bit down that day, worried about something. The kid didn't know what and Lenny didn't say, so he took his money and left. That was it."

"You don't think he was covering up, that he knew how to spin a good yarn?"

"Look, anything is possible. But if you ask me, I'd say no, the guy wasn't fudging it. He's a drop out, a street kid who hustles. Not a violent type, doesn't own a gun, hasn't been in knife fights, nothing like that. And believe me, he's no quiz kid. He doesn't have the *seckel* to rig up a phony hanging. If he actually had killed Lenny in a fit of rage, he'd have panicked and gotten out of there on the double. And he'd have left clues. No, I can't see him as a murderer."

"That leaves suicide. That's your conclusion?"

"Right now it looks that way. Your brother must have struggled with horrible guilt his whole life. And with what we now know was going down at the Center, people attacking him, trying to get rid of him, it was all too much. He must have been tired of fighting and just wanted out."

Barney's words cut deep. Steiner, too, had diagnosed suicide and I had rejected that conclusion, needed to reject it out of hand, to block out that intolerable idea. Now Barney was bringing it back. Listening to him, I felt a stabbing pain in my midsection and with it the accusation that I wasn't there for Lenny, that I let him down. I turned to Barney, needed to share what I was feeling.

"If that's true, Barney, I'll never forgive myself. I didn't see who Lenny was and I did nothing to help him." The truth is, I didn't want to know. I didn't want to have to contend with that kind of problem."

"You are looking through a rear-view mirror," Barney put in, "asking yourself to have been a different person. I did the same when my kid got into trouble. Beat myself up for not preventing it. You helped me with that, showed me I was attacking myself for not being some kind of seer, some super-human being. How about taking some of your own medicine?"

I smiled and thanked Barney for reaching out to me, for being my shrink.

"When it comes to myself, I'm not the best patient," I said, "I'm going to work at it."

Barney gave me the thumbs up. Then we returned to what he'd reported.

"So, is that it?" I asked. Is this the end of the story? What do we do now, close up shop and chalk one up for the NYPD?"

"Possibly. We may very well have to. But we are not quite through yet."

"What do you mean?"

"There's one thing I want to check out. Probably will come to nothing, but I want to run it down. It's possible, as the clerk said, that someone else could have gotten up to Lenny's room, so I asked the kid if he saw anyone he didn't recognize handing around the hotel that day, a stranger, someone he'd never seen before. Right away he mentions a guy sitting in the lobby. Someone new. The fellow looked prosperous, so the kid hangs around in case he showed an interest in becoming a client."

"Is that something we care about? These kids are always cruising, looking for business."

"This man was dark-skinned. Definitely foreign. Our boy thought he might be Indian or from that part of the world."

"And you were thinking Arab."

"Right."

"And the Arab you were thinking of is named Ahmed."

"Great minds think alike."

"Or one has been infected with the wrong-headed thinking of the other."

"A possibility. This could be another one of Barney's famous off-the-wall ideas, but let's check it out. Do you happen to have a picture of Ahmed?"

I shook my head. "I don't think I ever had one."

"Do you think you could get one? A picture and some object that he's handled? By the time I got into Lenny's hotel room, they'd cleaned it. There were no prints. I also checked the Internet. He deliberately did not post a photo."

"How in the world do I do that, hide out in the O.R. and snap a picture before Ahmed gets his mask on?"

"Not a bad idea. And while you're at it, maybe you could swipe a used scalpel. Or, as Ahmed's former partner, you could ask him to pose for a photo for old time's sake."

"Ahmed may be an Arab, but he knows what *meshuga* means. He'd think I've finally gone over the edge."

"Well I've got faith in you, Doc. I know you can find a way. And when you have that picture, I'll run it by our favorite hustler. Who knows, we might just get a hit."

At that point I told Barney about my meeting with Ahmed, about the connection we'd made.

As he listened, his spirits seemed to rise. He was back to his old self, seeing possibilities.

"Keep up your contact," he said. "Keep talking with him, and, more important, keep listening. The man wants to tell you his story. That's what we want. The more he talks, the more likely he'll tell us something we want to know."

"And you might just win this week's Power Ball lottery. And how were you planning to reward the kid for being our star witness?"

"I'll give him Ahmed's phone number."

I didn't laugh, I was cast down by Barney's news. I was sure that we were through, that Barney just didn't want to tell me. He must have read my mind. He reached out and touched my shoulder.

"Remember, Doc," he said, "the game is not over until the fat lady sings."

So we were still in business according to Barney, and I still had my meeting with the woman, Laura, coming up.

I remained puzzled about her, about her involvement with Ahmed, so I turned the conversation to my question about her.

Barney's response surprised me. The old gumshoe knew his Bard.

"An educated fellow like you in the profession you're in knows the answer to that," he said. "You see it every day. The lunatic and the lover are a package deal. There's no separation. The lady must have met your friend under a full moon."

And about my meeting with Laura, his advice was simple.

"Stick to your brother and his work with her boy. Don't let her know that you're interested in Ahmed. If she cottons to what you're up to, that you are using her to get info on her boyfriend, she'll clam up and make a beeline to warn him. At that point, my friend, we pack it in. You go back to your *mashuga* clients and I go back to daytime soap operas and the off-limit yogurt stand."

"I get it," I said. "But when I meet with this Laura lady I'll need you to send me thought waves, make sure my feet don't start moving in the wrong direction."

"Not to worry, partner," Barney said, "just ignore any strange feelings in those toesies of yours. That's just me doing my job."

Chapter 6

Laura's office was in a corner of the library. It was just before 1:00p.m. when I knocked on her door.

"Be with you in a minute, Doctor," she called out. "Just finishing up something."

A few minutes later, she invited me in. She was seated behind a desk that appeared not much bigger than student size. As I entered, she rose to greet me. She was wearing a lemon-yellow blouse and navy slacks. Her reddish-brown hair was pulled back off her face and fastened with a colorful barrette. She looked youthful, quite lovely. She started toward me.

"Have you had lunch yet, Doctor? I'm starved. There's a hole-in-the-wall canteen in the lobby. You can get a sandwich and coffee. Would you mind if we got something and brought it back here? Would that be alright?"

"Fine with me. It's past my lunchtime."

We took the stairs down two flights, bought sandwiches—tuna for me—egg salad for Laura—from a concession stand that seemed to be expertly carved into the rear wall of the lobby, and returned to her office. She resumed her place behind the desk and motioned for me to take the stolid, rather ugly classroom-type chair at her side.

She took a bite of sandwich, then a long look at me.

"So you are Leonard's brother and Ahmed's old friend?"

"I am." I smiled my best smile.

"I mentioned to Ahmed that we'd met," she said," he had a lot of good things to say about you. Said you were his surgical partner."

I laughed. "If he calls the robot who stood at the table and held the retractor a partner, I guess I was," I replied.

She smiled. Her voice was friendly, forthcoming.

"I'm not exaggerating, Doctor," she insisted, "Ahmed said you were a mean man with a scalpel, that you had good hands, but that you were bullheaded and insisted on becoming a shrink. And that you were lucky to have met him because he taught you all you know about dreams."

"So he's made sure to inform me a few thousand times," I responded. "He wants to make sure I have that straight. Ahmed Aslam is a great surgeon who has done some amazing things, but he'll tell you his greatest accomplishment is to have published a paper on dreams."

Now she laughed. "I know, I've heard that a few thousand times myself. It has to do with his father having written that paper with him. It meant a great deal to him that his dad invited him to do that."

"I realize that. His father was his hero and for good reason, Doctor Aslam was a distinguished scholar, the first person in his part of the world to have translated a number of Freud's papers into Arabic. Also, from all I've heard, a thoroughly good man who devoted much of his life to working for peace between Arabs and Jews."

"That's what I understand."

So what happened to Ahmed is what I wanted to say, but I kept my mouth shut.

Laura seemed to read my mind.

"His father's death was a crushing blow," she added. She said nothing about how he died, but I knew what she meant.

For a moment she looked away, overcome with feeling. Then she brightened, forced a smile.

"So you want to know about your brother's work," she said. "It would take a dozen of these meetings to do justice to Mr. Leonard Strickman. Your brother was a remarkably complex man, dedicated, fascinating, and incredibly difficult. He saved my boy's life and confused the hell out of him. With me, he gave me hope when I had none and drove me nuts with his stubbornness. And I wasn't alone. Lenny managed to alienate almost everyone here and a lot of people were out to get him."

I wanted to ask if that included Ahmed, but I remembered Barney's words about not bringing him into the conversation, so I held back.

"Sounds like things got pretty heated," is what I did say.

"You have no idea. Ahmed got so agitated by your brother's behavior, by his refusal to give an inch, that I honestly thought he was going to stroke out. And it wasn't only his anger that worried me. For some reason he feared Lenny. Your brother had some kind of mystical power over him that he could not shed. The only thing that released him was Lenny's death."

"Anyway, the situation became unbearable," Laura was saying, "Marco was pulled between Ahmed and Lenny, and half the time the child was in tears trying to deal with them. The situation was totally exhausting.. I was a complete wreck.

"Finally, I stepped in. I told Ahmed that this idiocy had to stop, that it was hurting too many people. I told him that he needed to find a solution and that the only way to do that was to meet Lenny man-to-man someplace away from the Center, away from all the hostility and hatred, and work something out."

"And did Ahmed listen to you?"

"Actually, I think he did. He didn't say much, just kept his mad face on, but I know he heard me. Ahmed has a fierce temper. He can lash out with the best of them, but he's not vicious, not like some radicals.

He has a heart and he does not want to hurt innocent people. He loves Marco and I think he loves me, too. So, yes, I think he did listen."

What Laura reported, the information she provided, was exactly what I was after. She had given me reason to believe that Barney's hunch might be on target, that the man in the lobby of the Pearl could very well have been Ahmed. If that were true, clearly he was not there to make peace. The fact that my brother's body was found strangled in a bathtub the next day made the link between his presence in the hotel and the murder all but certain. I could not allow myself to push away what now seemed evident, that Ahmed had come to eliminate his enemy, to silence someone he despised and who had the power to bring him down, to destroy him and the mission he was committed to carry out.

At that point, I wanted to ask Laura more questions about Ahmed's attitude and behavior, but something—perhaps it was Barney sending me thought messages—told me that this was not the time to pursue her with questions that could put her on guard, cause her to shut down, and eliminate our chances of using her as a source for the future.

So I changed the subject. I asked her about herself, her background, how she happened to come to the Center. I wanted to show interest, to build a relationship.

Laura was eager to talk. She seemed to have a need to unburden herself.

"My route to this place was a pretty thorny one," she said. "At the age of forty-five, I found myself alone in life, a single mother with a troubled child. I didn't know where to turn.

"I had made a horrible marriage, was divorced and thoroughly traumatized. I wanted the high life, and when I met my ex I fooled myself into believing that he would provide it; money, travel, adventure, all of it. But, of course, it was all make believe. Robert turned out to be a clever manipulator. For some reason, he decided he wanted me in his life and he knew how to play his cards. He flooded me with attention and I was naïve. I took his declarations of love for the real thing. But it didn't take long to realize that the only person Robert could love was himself.

"He also turned out to be a shyster, a con man who smooth talked old ladies into investing with him. Not only did he lose their money, he made himself rich by charging exorbitant fees.. In the end, he got investigated by the DA and narrowly escaped a prison term.

"You can imagine how miserable I was, Doctor. I was married to a psychopath and had no children. I was going to divorce the son of a bitch but he swore he'd learned his lesson and was determined to change. He said that he now wanted children and to live as a family man. And idiot that I am, I believed him. I had trouble conceiving, so we decided to adopt. We could have done it the usual way, privately or through an agency, but that was too bourgeois for me. I wanted the dramatic; to rescue a child, save him from a life of misery, do something for humanity."

"You adopted from Brazil?"

"You heard about that? I guess Ahmed told you about Marco. Did he tell you that his father abandoned the kid, that after swearing up and down that he wanted children, he simply took off after a couple of years. Said he'd had enough. So he just split."

I nodded. "I heard. How awful for you."

"Never mind me. It's Marco who really got hurt. Abandoned for the second time. And just when he was allowing himself to get attached to his father.

"You have no idea what it's been like. My life has been consumed by one thing, and one thing only; taking care of a troubled child. Frankly, I don't know how I've kept on. There is no way I could have without help. Thank God for Ahmed and Mohammed. They have been real bricks, always ready to help out when I needed them."

Her saying that caused a bolt of jealousy to rip at my insides, and with it a surge of anger. What exactly is so great about Ahmed and his bigoted sidekicks, I felt like asking, but I kept my mouth shut. Old feelings of rivalry with Ahmed were surfacing; I'd always envied his skills and his attractiveness to women. And now, I realized, this was playing out in relation to Laura. I wanted her to be drawn to me, to find me more appealing than Ahmed.. I was tempted to say something critical about him, to put him down, but I managed to catch myself, and hold back.

Fortunately, Laura changed the subject. She wanted to know about me.

"I'm a lucky guy," I said. "I've drawn the long straw. I have a fascinating profession, a great wife, and two kids who I live for. "I am lucky, too, to have good friends. I know what you mean when you say how important that is."

At that point I talked about Ahmed and our time together as a team. I wanted Laura to know that we were close, how much I respected him. I described several of the cases we worked on and how, if it wasn't for Ahmed's skill and perseverance, the patients, all teenagers, would not have survived.

I played down the fights we got into, the way we went head-to-head over the Israeli-Palestinian wars and how intransigent Ahmed was. I did not want her to get the idea that I had come to the Center to find out if his hatred had turned poisonous, if bitterness had eroded his soul, turned him into someone the Ahmed I knew, the old Ahmed, would not himself have recognized.

"Ahmed is not an easy man," Laura put in. "You know that. When he's particularly difficult, I try to keep in mind what he's been through. He appreciates that, appreciates the effort I make. And that you must make, too."

I nodded. What Laura was saying about Ahmed, I, too, experienced. That there were times when one had to dig down deep to find empathy for him. But in saying what she did, I thought she was also expressing a wish that someone understand her, understand what she'd been through, the way she tried to understand Ahmed.

I wanted to reach out to her, to help her through this dark time and find a better path for her and her boy.

We said goodbye and arranged to meet again. She had more to tell me, Laura said. I sensed that this was not only about my brother, but about herself. She had a need to talk, to tell her own story, to share her pain and her hope that as a shrink I might understand.

As for me, talking about Ahmed the way I did, telling stories about the two of us and our work together, brought up memories. I so missed those days, the caring friendship we had, missed the Ahmed I knew; mourned him, just as I mourned my dear brother.

It was William Faulkner, I think, who said the past is not gone , it is not even past.

I often thought of that as I worked with patients whose lives continued to be decisively influenced by their need to enact old scripts, old scenarios. But I never had experienced a true revival of the past, the replay of an old forgotten scenario. And yet the very next day that is what happened—or seemed to. Time reversed itself, long forgotten scenes surfaced, and the old Ahmed reappeared; that is, until reality broke through, the new Ahmed barged in, and the past vanished into the mist of a raw and chilly new day.

Chapter 7

It happened when I was at the hospital. I had a half-hour break between the two halves of my weekly stint; supervising a resident on his psychotherapy case and conducting a continuous case seminar, so I called Barney to report on my meeting with Laura.

He was full of praise.

"Great work, Doc," he said. "The boys' downtown will be proud of you. You handled the lady beautifully. Got her talking and she gave you what we needed. Odds are it was Ahmed in the lobby, waiting for a chance to slip upstairs and wrap his belt around your brother's neck. When you finish the job, we'll be in business."

I had no idea what the man was talking about—until I remembered. The picture and the DNA. My latest assignment; to come up with a photo of Ahmed and a sample of his DNA. But just how I was to do this my partner had neglected to inform me. So I had conveniently repressed the whole matter. Not that I underestimated the importance of collecting evidence. But I was less than enthusiastic about the prospect of tying my guts into spastic knots in an effort to carry out a task that I could think of no way of accomplishing.

I was about to call Barney and inform him that after thinking things over I realized that as the brains of our outfit and our senior strategist, he was eminently more qualified than I to handle this challenging project, when the loudspeaker on the floor erupted and a woman's voice broke through the static on the line.

"Attention, attention. All medical and nursing personnel report immediately to the Emergency Room."

Almost instantly the unit emptied out. Everyone on duty headed for the stairs and within minutes had joined the crowd outside the E.R. The place was in pandemonium. A gunman had broken into a Jewish day school and had fired wildly into several classrooms before turning the gun on himself. Five children had been killed and more than a dozen wounded. The victims had arrived in ambulances and police cars and were carried into a triage unit. The dead were transported to the hospital morgue. Those wounded but still alive were examined, and if judged salvageable, readied for surgery. Many in critical condition, however, had to wait for an O.R. to open up. All the hospital had were quickly occupied.

The call had gone out to every surgeon on the staff to come in as quickly as possible. I looked for Ahmed. I did not see him. I asked a nurse if she had seen Dr. Aslam.

"Don't think he's come in," she replied.

I asked a couple of residents. Neither had seen Ahmed. The HYC was ;just two miles from the hospital, so that it would have taken Ahmed a matter of minutes to arrive.

I found myself feeling bitter.

No doubt he had called in, I thought, and when he learned that a Jewish school had been attacked, he chose not to come in. That was his protest, his revenge. I imagined him thinking, 'Now they know what it is like. Perhaps now they will understand what the Israelis did to us, how our children suffered. Well, let them experience suffering of their own. It is long overdue.' And so he had decided not to respond, just as Jewish doctors often failed to respond to the suffering of Arab children. How unworthy of him, I thought to myself. Ahmed, the great surgeon, who has always maintained that first and foremost he was a physician, that when it came to treating patients he set politics aside, had demonstrated the emptiness of those fine words. He had chosen loyalty to his tribe, his identity as an Arab, over his pledge to treat without discrimination all who sought his help. I recalled what Alice had said; that Ahmed was a man bent on revenge. Well now he had gotten it. He had his pound of flesh.

I was in an alcove off the E.R. trying to comfort a young girl on a gurney who had suffered a leg wound when one of the surgeons popped his head it.

"Hear you were looking for Dr. Aslam," he said. "He' was here but no O.R. was open so he took one of the kids across the way to the ambulatory building. The child couldn't wait for surgery,"

"Thanks."

My face flushed. I turned away so no one could see me.

"When a nurse came in to take my place with the injured child, I made my way across a courtyard to the low, two-story Ambulatory Care building. It contained a small operating room on the first floor.

I took a seat on a bench a short distance from the O.R. doors and waited. Across the room a middle-aged Hasidic couple were seated on an identical bench. They sat close together and were murmuring to one another. At intervals the husband stood, walked to the picture window at the rear of the room, looked out briefly, and returned.

We remained that way, sitting in silence, not acknowledging one another for about half an hour. Then the O.R. doors opened and Ahmed appeared, closely followed by a scrub nurse.

As he emerged, Ahmed removed his gloves, threw them in a bin for used materials, and approached the couple across the room. They rose to meet him, but he motioned them to sit and he sat alongside them. He talked with them for a good twenty minutes, speaking in a low voice, calmly, explaining everything he had done, reassuring them that all had gone well and that their daughter would make a full recovery.

The mother took Ahmed's hand in hers.

"Thank you, thank you, doctor," she said. "You are a wonderful person, a life-saver." The father nodded, reached out and touched Ahmed's shoulder, a small gesture of gratitude.

The scene was familiar to me. I had witnessed many like it in the years Ahmed and I worked together. He never spoke of them, never looked for thanks. He just did his job. I admired him for that, admired the man he was.

I remained that way for a few more minutes, sitting alone, remembering. Then I forced myself to think about Ahmed, not the man of the past, but the man who, out of bitterness, and a need for vengeance, had aligned himself with a bunch of ruthless killers.

Then I recalled my assignment; the photo and the DNA. Now I felt an urge to obtain them, to do my job and bring them to Barney. And not only to display my skill, my ingenuity. I needed something tangible for myself; evidence, proof of Ahmed's involvement; a way to provide clarity, to dispel the confusion that was racking my brain.

The DNA, it turned out, presented no problem. All I needed was to get hold of the gloves Ahmed had discarded. This I did by sidling up to the waste bin, wrapping a hand in tissue, and when no one was looking, slipping a glove of his—I noticed that his gloves were on the very top of the discarded materials—into my pocket.

The photo was another matter. There was no way, out of the blue, that I could snap a picture of Ahmed or ask him to pose for one without appearing to have gone off the rails. And Ahmed was no fool. He would know immediately that I was up to something. He would have all kinds of questions and I had no answers.

I was stumped and was about to accept defeat when something flashed into my mind. I looked at Ahmed and the Hasidic couple. They were standing now, and Ahmed was giving them instructions about their daughter's post-operative care. On impulse I approached the three of them. I introduced myself to the parents as Dr. Aslam's colleague. I said I was aware of their situation and how much Dr. Aslam had helped them.

"You people have been through a horrific day," I said, "but it looks as though it is going to be alright thanks to this wonderful doctor here. It occurred to me that you might like to have a picture of yourself with him. I have my cell phone right here."

Ahmed stared at me and shook his head, signaling me to stay away. But he was too late.

"That would be awfully nice of you," the mother replied. "We would be very grateful."

"Thank you, doctor," the husband added.

Ahmed was trapped. He had to stand next to the couple while I took two quick photos, which I showed them.

"Very nice," the mother said. "You'll send us a copy?"

"Leave your name and address at the desk before you leave and I'll have a copy in the mail," I promised. Ahmed was fuming quietly. I knew he hated to be made a fuss over and, especially, to have pictures taken of him. Furthermore, I was holding him up from attending to other patients who urgently needed care. I knew that he would have liked nothing better than to punch me out, but he could do nothing but smile, take my cell phone when I handed it to him, and pretend to appreciate the photo I had taken.

Then, giving me a dirty look, he said goodbye to the parents, invited them to call him, and walked away. He said nothing to me.

In less than a minute I headed for the exit and reached the street. I did not want to be anywhere near Ahmed. I had no interest in being the target of the kind of angry outburst that I'd seen him deliver to colleagues who he regarded as hopeless blockheads. He had no tolerance for stupidity and, besides, I did not want to have to make up some idiotic explanation. I was afraid the guilt I felt would trip me up and I would blow everything.

I was no more than a block away from the hospital when they bombarded me; images of what I had just seen, of what I could no longer bear to see; small bodies torn apart, pale, lifeless children, parents clutching one another, praying, weeping. And with those images came a burning rage; rage and a wish to destroy the Arab—witnesses described him as praising Allah as he mowed down children—who had committed this barbaric act.

I was about half-way home when my phone rang. It was Ahmed and he was angry. He did not waste words.

"Siggie, I don't want my picture floating around out there. Please destroy it at once."

"Your picture is not floating around anywhere. I have it on my phone and the only people I'll share it with are the parents you were speaking with."

"That's all very good, but I don't know what they will do with it. I don't want it out there."

"They were so happy to take a photo with you. It won't do any harm to let them have it. It means a lot to them."

"Look, Siggie, I am not arguing with you. Either you destroy that picture, or I'll have to do it for you."

"Calm down, Ahmed. You are making something out of nothing. It's an Iphone photo. That's it. These folks will keep it on their mantel for the next thirty years. There's no problem here."

He didn't answer. He'd hung up.

I kept walking, Ahmed's angry voice in my ears, my head starting to throb.

I was almost home, five or six blocks away, when I had the uneasy feeling that I was being followed. I stopped in front of a store window, waited a moment, looked behind me. No one. Nothing. A few pedestrians, nothing suspicious. But the feeling persisted, a sense that something was up, that I was in danger.

I walked another block, stopped suddenly, turned, and that is when I saw it; a black van a dozen yards behind, moving slowly, keeping pace with me. I ducked into a bodega. I walked to the rear and concealed myself behind a line of customers. Then I reached for my phone and sent the picture of Ahmed and the parents to Barney. I didn't know if I would make it home. Barney needed that photo.

I waited ten minutes, then walked out. The van was in front of the store. I had barely cleared the entranceway when Abdul was on me. Springing from the van, he lunged at me, grabbed me around the neck, pinned me against the storefront window. Then he drove the flat of his hand into my collar bone. I fell hard, striking my head against the base of the window. Pain ripped through my head and neck. Everything blurred. I could not focus. Abdul stood over me, tugged at my jacket, my trousers. My phone tumbled out. He grabbed it and stuffed it into a pocket.

"Don't ever pull that kind of shit again," he shouted. "Ahmed told us about your little stunt. Try that shit with us, and we'll have your ass. This was a warning. Next time we'll mean business."

To emphasize his point, he administered a hard kick to my ribs. An electric charge flashed through my body. I could not breathe. Abdul surveyed his handy work for a moment, then turned and walked back to the van. As it took off, I caught a glimpse of Mohammed at the wheel.

I made it home—slowly—called Barney and told him what had happened. A few minutes later, he rang the bell. When he saw me holding my side, still in pain, his face flushed and he punched at the air.

"Those *momsers*," he muttered. "Fuckers. Thugs, all of them, cowards. The good Doctor too. He must have sent them after you."

"I don't know. Those two act on their own. They don't seem to trust Ahmed."

"Why should they? He's got a Jewish girlfriend. Before you know it, he'll be keeping Kosher. But don't kid yourself, all of them are killers. If you had put up a fight, right now you'd be lying under a sheet in that doorway. That creep would have thought nothing of putting a bullet in your head."
"He didn't need a gun. He nearly did me in as is."

"That was just round one, Doc. You have plenty of juice left."
"I do?"

"Absolutely. With Barney in your corner, next time you'll knock the stuffing out of those scarecrows."

"How about me being in your corner and you knocking the stuffing out of them?"

"Doesn't work that way, Doc. Right now we have a great set up. You are our inside man going toe to toe with those low life's, and me behind you, backing you up all the way. With foreign types like these, it's best to use the 23rd's playbook. Our guys deal with *gonifs* from every corner of the globe, and handle them with our PMA approach."

"What's that?"

"We use mental jujitsu and Tai Kwando to get one up on the perps, followed with verbal feints to get under their defenses. Then we use their own blockhead thinking to bring them down."

"Brilliant. I can't wait to learn the system. But I have a hunch Abdul and company may have stolen your formula. He had me off balance and on the ground before I could pronounce his name."

"Not to worry. I'll teach you everything. In a couple of weeks, you'll be right up there with the best PMA men. If this Abdul makes another move on you, he'll be on his back before he can pronounce his own name."

Buoyed by Barney's optimism and feeling a good deal better, I produced the discarded glove that that I had wrapped in tissue and stuffed into a jacket pocket. Barney was delighted.

"Great thinking, Doc. I'm putting you up for the most improved gumshoe of the month."

"Terrific. What's the prize, a complete First Aid kit?"

"Better. A half dozen fully paid visits to the Urgent Care of your choice."

Barney's words did not do much to improve my state of mind. The confusion I had experienced had not left me. Everything we knew now pointed to Ahmed as our man. Laura had openly acknowledged his hatred of Lenny and that he desired nothing more than to throttle the life out of him. We had our motive. And the gloves and the DNA could very well place Ahmed at the scene of the crime. Everything was falling into place.

But still I felt uneasy. Images of Ahmed sitting with the Hasidic couple kept surfacing in my mind. This was the old Ahmed, the Ahmed I knew and admired. He was still here. But was he the only Ahmed with us? Was there another Ahmed, one in league with the Arab who murdered innocent children? Again, pictures of what I had just seen invaded me; hurt and dying children lying on gurneys; silent in their pain. And with those memories came something else. A wish for vengeance that I had never known before.

Chapter 8

Barney and I arranged to meet the next day to discuss Abdul's surprise attack and to plan our strategy for the days ahead. Barney suggested the Lenox Avenue Deli, a popular spot not far from the Center, but I was not happy with that choice.

"They get a crowd from HYC at lunchtime." I said. "I don't want some busybody listening in on us."

"Not to worry, Doc. That gang is so busy stuffing their faces, they wouldn't notice if the Ayatollah sat down at the next table. Probably think he was La Toya's new hire."

"I do worry. After yesterday's gambit, Ahmed's bound to be suspicious. He and his geek friends are going to be watching our every move. Wherever we go, you can bet they won't be far behind."

"If they follow us to the Deli, we'll spot them. My radar can detect *traif* eaters from thirty yards away."

"Thank God for that. There is nothing worse than being ambushed by infidels like that."

When we got to the Deli the next day, it was packed, as usual, but we found a small table in the rear. After our waiter poured two glasses of seltzer, the management's version of *Amuse bouche*, Barney broke the news.

"Ahmed's our man," he announced.

"You got a hit?"

"A bull's eye. The kid made a positive ID from the photo, no question. Knew Ahmed right away. Same with the desk clerk. Both were sure he was the man in the lobby. And not only that, Doc, I found a chambermaid who saw Ahmed in Lenny's room. She'll swear it was him. A genuine eye-witness."

Barney explained that the maid came to turn down Lenny's bed the evening before his body was found.

"She knocks," he said, "gets no answer, so uses her pass key to let herself in. And there they are, sitting face to face, Lenny and another man. I show her the photo and she fingers him right away. It's Ahmed. The two are arguing. When she comes back the next morning, your brother is sprawled out in the bathtub, a belt around his neck. Doesn't get much clearer than that."

Barney had convincing material. And what he had uncovered went along with what Laura had told me at one point; that Ahmed knew Lenny was staying in a hotel. I told Barney what she said.

"There you go. That clinches it. Our man, Ahmed, had the motivation and the opportunity and was spotted at the scene of the crime. We are nearly ready to talk to Steiner."

"I guess so."

I had to agree. We now had almost enough to bring to him, but I found it hard to get the words out. Something in me rebelled, wanted to say no, your facts, your evidence, are not the same as the truth. But that would sound idiotic, irrational. What Barney said was right; bringing evidence enough for Steiner to reopen the case was what we were aiming for. But the fact that all we had pointed to Ahmed seemed wrong, a betrayal. And I couldn't shake the heaviness, the feeling of despair that came over me.

Barney read my face and immediately understood.

"I know what you are thinking," he said. "This is not possible. It doesn't compute. The man who saved the life of a Hasidic child, could not be the man in the hotel lobby, waiting for the right moment to get upstairs and hang your brother by the neck. I don't know Ahmed the way you do, Doc, but I feel the same way. This just couldn't be. Human beings are not made like that."

"That's what kept me up half the night. Thinking and getting nowhere, coming up with *bupkus*, nothing but pains in the kishkes. Things got so bad, I just lost it. A pint of Chobani nonstop. Unbelievable, I know. I didn't believe it myself. Don't tell my wife. If she finds out, she'll call the suicide hotline. They are liable to contact the cops and my choice will be abstinence or the psych ward at Bellevue."

"Your secret is safe with me, Barney, I'll never tell."

"You're a pal, Doc. Anyway, *fressing* didn't work, so I tried the *schvitz* technique, sweating it out in the bathtub. And know what? While I was in there soaking like my mother's brisket, I had an idea. No brainstorm, no big ticket item, just a thought, really."

"That's more than I have."

"Okay. See what you think. I'm figuring the radio transcript put us on the right track. Lenny had something big on Ahmed and his boys, so he had to be eliminated. They found out about the Pearl and Lenny's gay life, so they came up with the idea of faking a suicide. But they needed a back-up plan in case that one doesn't fly. So Ahmed got the job because everyone knows he has it in for Lenny and if things go wrong and the cops wise up, they'll come after him."

I saw where Barney was going.

"And the others can remain under cover so their operation won't get broken up."

"Right. You've got a good *kup* on you, Doc."

"And you, too, my friend. What you're saying makes a lot of sense. I can see that Ahmed would be the choice for designated killer. Except for one thing. We don't know if he's capable of killing."

"He is," Barney said. "Definitely. That's what came to me at four in the morning. Or, rather, came to my wife. I'm lying there, not *schluffing*, and in my ear I hear her giving advice. 'Look at the obvious, Barney,' she's telling me. 'Look at what's in front of your nose.'

I was not sure why she's saying that, but it's Doris, she who must be obeyed, so I do what she's telling me and I ask myself what's most obvious about our man Ahmed,. The answer, of course, is that he's a dedicated doctor. That's what you keep saying. He's a doctor, he saves lives, he doesn't take them. And then it hit me. The two of us have been staring at one side of a two-sided coin. Turn it over and it's the same coin, but an entirely different look.

"I'm being thick, Barney. I'm not following you."

"It's me, Doc, I'm being obtuse, like my wife says. When she first called me that, I got insulted, thought she was saying I'm a fatso, but I finally got the message. I explain everything crystal clear to myself, and nobody else can understand me. Let me try this way. What do doctors do? They save lives, try to beat the game of death. That's what they are about. But they also have to put up with death, even bring it on. You and Ahmed worked in an E.R. You did triage. Some patients you saved, others were too far gone. You had to let them go. So those people you condemned to death.

"And you've done research. What happens when a new drug is discovered? It goes through trials, is given to some sick patients, not to others just as sick. If it is a lifesaver, the ones who get it live, many of the others die.

"Doctors accept that because it is for a higher cause. Ultimately, to save lives. As a surgeon who spent half his life in E.R.s, Ahmed is very familiar with this thinking. He lives with it. It's part of him. So, it was not hard for him to accept the idea that for Isis' cause to prevail, the enemies of Allah must be eliminated. It's the same basic idea he's accepted, only transported to the fight for Arab rights.

"The regular Joe's who join Isis and get brainwashed become total converts. They take on the way of thinking and the Jihad way of life of their captors. They become blind soldiers in that cause. They lose who they were, abandon their former selves. Ahmed can't do that. Being a doctor, a healer, is too deep in him. No brainwashing can undo that, so what he does is split himself, but not like doubles with two different personalities, one hidden from the other. No, the split is between two sets of beliefs, two loyalties. He is first and foremost the doctor who seeks to heal, to save lives. But if he gets the call from on high to carry out Jihad, to take the life of an enemy, he can do that because killing now serves a higher purpose. It is in the interest of freeing people from bondage."

I was impressed with my partner. He saw what I could not see. And he was right. I was fixated on just one side of a two-sided coin. It never occurred to me to turn it over.

"Congratulations, Barney," I said. "The day you turned in your badge was a sad one for the 23rd. They lost a great mind."

Barney turned to face me and did a little bow.

"Thank you, my friend," he said. "Your words are much appreciated. But it's my wife who deserves the thanks. She's the one who made me look at what was right in front of my schnozola."

"But we haven't crossed the finish line yet," he added. "We still have a ways to go. What we have is good, but it's circumstantial. We need the hard stuff, proof that will convince a jury. That's what Steiner will want before he makes a move."

"How are we going to get that?"

"With a sting operation, Mossad-style. We had an Israeli connection at the 23rd. One of our men made *Aliyah*, joined Mossad, and shared some of their tactics with us. They specialize in planting informers among Arab radicals. We nabbed a lot of mob members doing the same thing."

"So, you are going undercover as a Jihadist? No offense, Barney, but it will take a lot of fancy footwork to pull that off."

"Too fancy for me, Doc, but luckily for me I have a partner who knows all the right moves."

I did not like the sound of this. I had a sudden urge to ask for the check. Barney read my feelings.

"Not to worry, Doc, you are a perfect fit for this job. How is your acting ability?"

"Rotten. My last performance was as Pinocchio in a camp play and I was criticized for being too wooden."

"Well, here's your chance to redeem yourself, make a brilliant comeback. And your role is an easy one. You're a convert, a Palestinian supporter. You've seen the light, finally heard what Ahmed has been saying all these years. You heard about his father, how such a good man, a man who worked for peace, was killed by the Israeli's. You realized how brutal Israel has become. And you've talked with Marco's mother, Ahmed's lady friend. She described her work with the Palestinians, all the suffering she witnessed. She's been a strong influence. And you know Ahmed, what will reach him, what he'd want to hear from you."

"I'd need an operation to pull that act off. Can you arrange a quick Laurence Olivier transplant?"

"Not needed, Doc. You actually have a lot of experience acting. Haven't you been playing a role for years; the cool, objective psychoanalyst?"

"I was pretty bad at that, Barney. I had to give it up. My patients saw through me."

"Well, you'll be convincing with Ahmed because down deep you know that there's a lot of truth in what he says."

"That may be, but I don't think I can get out the words you are asking me to speak. I'll choke on them, and if I do manage to get them out, my brother will be out of his grave and deck me before I finish a sentence."

"Lenny will understand. He knows how Massad operates, how they use informers who live as Arabs, pray five times a day, curse Israel, do the whole bit to get the info they need. And he'd approve of what we're doing. He knows we're trying to prevent a disaster. Don't think these people will stop at one murder. You can bet the house that they are planning attacks that will kill hundreds of innocent people."

"You're probably right, but I'd feel a lot better if I could explain that to my brother. Do you know anyone who runs a good séance?"

"As a matter of fact, I have an aunt in the business. She has a specialty; strictly Orthodox séances. The men wear yarmulkes and the women sit in another room. She's been endorsed by the Council of Orthodox Rabbis."

"See if you can sign her up. Knowing that Lenny understands what we're doing and that it's okay with him would make things a lot easier. I feel all alone in this.

"Not to worry. I'll be out there with you, doing my thing."

"Which is what, imitating the Mossad approach, New York style?"

Barney nodded, "Not only imitating, improving. I'll be adding a few tricks of my own, courtesy of the 23rd. You'll introduce me to LaToya as a retired bookkeeper you met at your gym. We got to schmoozing and I let you know that time hangs on my hands like a butcher shop salami and that I was looking for what to do. You mentioned the Center, what good work goes on there, and I got interested in coming on board. Since Lenny is gone, and LaToya will need help with the books, it shouldn't be too hard to talk my way in. Once I'm inside, I'll nose around, see if I can pick up what's going on. If someone is cooking the books, I think I'll be able to sniff out the scheme. I've got a good nose for *gonifs*."

"Terrific. We should be a great team. Billy and Barney, AKA, Laurel and Hardy."

"Don't knock us, Doc. We are on the case, definitely making headway. Just think where we were a few days ago, strictly *gornisht*, two empty heads without a clue. Now we are in business, mounting a sting operation that will give us some answers."

"I don't know what I'd do without you, Barney. You are my staff and my support."

"Likewise, Doc," Barney said.

We were walking out together when I spotted them, Abdul and Mohammed, a few tables away, huddled with two of the Muslim staff. I hadn't noticed them come in, but now, as we started for the door, I could see them watching us. I nudged Barney and he nodded.

"Where are you headed now?" he murmured.

"To my office. I have a patient coming in half an hour."

"Enough time to walk there?"

"I'm ten minutes away."

"Okay. You start out. I'm going to follow half a block behind. I want to see if I'm paranoid or if I picked up a signal, something between those two friends of yours. It was the way they exchanged looks."

"What kind of looks?"

"Sneaky glances. Furtive, as they say in detective stories. But it might have been nothing, my imagination working overtime. I've been known to arrest people on the street who looked at me cross-eyed. You just keep walking, not too fast, though. This Chobani belly makes it a bit hard to keep up. And, anyway, you don't want our lunch companions to think they've managed to scare you away."

Once out the door, I assumed a nonchalant shopper's stroll and ambled in the direction of a line of stores at the end of the street. When I reached them, I stopped and perused the windows for a couple of minutes. I didn't look back.

About a block from my office, I stopped at a curb to wait for a red light before crossing a busy intersection. When the light changed and I started forward, a black van that I'd noticed also waiting at the light turned sharply, cut in front of me, its grill passing less than a foot from my legs, and sped away, its gunned motor making a deafening sound. I retreated to the curb and waited for Barney

"Did you see that?" I asked when he caught up with me. He nodded.

"Abdul said it. These people mean business."

"What do we do now?"

"Right now, nothing. Ignore them. They are trying to drive you away."

"And they are doing a damn good job of it."

"We haven't begun to fight," Barney said, "once we get our operation rolling, these people will be sorry they ever started with us. They'll be squirming in our net like a bunch of hooked blowfish."

"Speak for yourself."

"Just don't allow yourself to be bullied. That's what they want. Just go about your business."

"I've got an anxious patient to see right now. I don't know who is going to be more of a basket case, him or me."

"Not to worry. Our strategy will have them just where we want them."

"From your mouth to Jehovah's ear."

For the rest of the way to my office, I did deep breathing and managed to calm down a bit—until I got there.

On my answering machine there were three hang-ups in a row—a rarity—followed by a message from a voice I did not recognize.

"Doctor, this is Georgette Connor from HYC. We haven't met, but I knew your brother. We worked together in accounting. He was a sweet man, very kind to me. People spoke against him, said nasty things, but to me he was a good man, someone who lived up to his religion.

"I was shocked to hear that he passed on. Just fell over, died on the spot, they say. Heart attack we're told. Condolences to you, by the way. People do drop dead, it's true. Happened to a cousin of mine, also a good man.

"Of course, I don't know what happened to Leonard—how could I know—but I'm calling you because I don't want anything to happen to you, even though I don't know you. But you are Leonard's brother. I think you understand what I'm saying."

My first impulse, then, was to contact Barney, tell him of the call, repeat what I'd heard. I wanted him with me, someone to talk to, to share my fear. I wanted to hear him say that he knew what was going on, that he had things under control, and that we were in no real danger. But I didn't call. I sat quietly for a moment, took a few more deep breaths, and opened the door to my office. It was pretty much a toss-up as to who was in worse shape, my patient or me, but I figured he had a slight edge. He needed me a tad more than I needed my partner. I was glad, though, that he was one of my patients who used the couch and didn't look at me. I didn't think at that moment that I inspired a lot of confidence.

Chapter 9

We were supposed to be equals in our partnership. We named our-selves the YF—for yogurt *Fressers*—Agency, but somehow Barney had a way of volunteering me as front man in any scheme he hatched.

As far as I was concerned, his latest ploy; casting me as a pro-Palestinian, was pure folly. My credentials as a thespian began and ended with my role as Pinocchio and if I was wooden then, how petrified would I be now?

Barney brushed away my fears. "You'll knock 'em dead, Doc," he said. "You know Ahmed's *schtick*. Just give it back to him. He'll be delighted to hear his fine sentiments coming out of your mouth. Before you know it, you'll be initiated into Hamas West, the club he's forming with his two buddies."

Usually Barney's words were encouraging. They buoyed my spirit. Now, though, they added to my fear that I would bomb horribly, humiliate myself, and put an end to Barney's scheme.

I need not have worried. The end, or what seemed like the end, came from another source.

I was in the middle of rehearsing my role in front of Alice, who was acting as audience and coach—at one point she commented that if things didn't work out, I could always get a gig playing a Palestinian on Saturday Night Live—whcn the phone rang. It was La Toya and she came right to the point. I was fired. Mohammed and Abdul had led a delegation to her office and demanded that I be barred from the Center. After what happened with my brother, they said, "allowing another Strickman to work there would spark a revolution."

"I cannot afford to have dissention among my staff," she said. "I'm sure you understand. I appreciate your offer to carry on Leonard's work, but under the circumstances, it's just not possible. I must ask you not to come here again."

"Does Dr. Aslam know about this?" I asked.

"I cannot discuss that with you," LaToya replied. And wishing me good luck, she hung up.

The fact that she refused to answer made me suspicious that Ahmed was behind this move.

LaToya's decision hit me hard. Without my having access to the Center, we would have no way to get the evidence we needed. And without that, Steiner would do nothing. Ahmed and Company had outsmarted us. I was miserable, feeling totally defeated.

Not Barney. When I broke the news to him, he responded immediately.

"The curtain is just going up," he said. "You're on stage. You are going to call Latoya back and put on your best Pinocchio performance. You are going to convince her that her people have it wrong. You are not Lenny and you don't endorse his views. In fact, you have come to agree completely with the staff. You are one hundred percent on their side. If she believes you can make peace and work things out without causing disruption, there's a good chance she will go along. The Center needs a shrink and LaToya knows how useful you can be. She'll want to believe you.

"Then it will be time for Act Two, convincing Ahmed and Company that you've seen the light, have become a convert, and are ready to join their fight against the Israeli brutes."

"I won't be able to pull that off." I said. "They'll spot my nose getting longer with every word I speak and LaToya will send me packing."

"Don't knock yourself," Barney said. "Promoting a sense of security is your thing. How do you think you're able to get people to sign up for five years on your couch? You do Honest Abe one better. Besides, I will be with you all the way, whispering in your ear if you get stuck."

That gave me as much comfort as having Yogi Berra as my personal teleprompter, but I said nothing to Barney. I merely told him that it was good to know I had a partner like him and that I would do my best.

In fact, I pulled it off. Or almost did. La Toya listened, was impressed by what I had to say, but remained skeptical.

"I tell you what, Doctor," she said by way of compromise, "speak to Doctor Aslam. If he thinks it is workable for you to be stay on, we'll can give it a try. But only as a trial. If there is any disruption, you'll have to leave."

Barney celebrated a victory. At my house he toasted with his favorite after dinner drink, Dr. Brown's cream soda, which he brought for the occasion.

"Great performance, Doc. You get this year's Arafat medal. You kept us in the game and that's what we needed."

I agreed but felt at a loss as to how to do that, how to become a member of Ahmed's team and pick up info from the inside.. I finally decided that Barney was right, I needed to play the convert, someone who has seen the light.

I told Ahmed that I'd been doing a lot of thinking and I'd come to appreciate what he'd been saying about Israel's brutality and the terrible suffering it had inflicted on the Palestinian people.

Ahmed replied that he was glad to hear it, that he had always regarded me as a person who honored the truth, and he knew that sooner or later I'd come around.

I took advantage of that moment to make my case for joining Ahmed's team. I pointed out how useful it would be to have a shrink readily available, especially since Marco was showing signs of regression and had slipped back into mutism.

Ahmed agreed, but nothing came of it. Never any follow up. He blamed Mohammed, claimed he was the stumbling block, that if I came on board he'd go to LaToya and threaten a revolution unless she got rid of me.

At one point he arranged a face-to-face meeting with Mohammed with the idea that a direct conversation would ease the tension between us.

It didn't happen.

Mohammed was opposed to the idea, but one afternoon, when I was in Ahmed's office, he brought him in, his hand at Mohammed's elbow like a principal forcing a recalcitrant bully to face his accuser. For several minutes Mohammed sat opposite me, totally silent, just staring at me with bone-chilling hostility. Finally he spoke.

"Your brother was a bigot," he said, "a bigot and a blind man. He shut his eyes to the truth, to the brutality of the Israelis. He refused to use the word, Occupation. He knew what was happening, the torture the Israeli were inflicting on us, but he refused to admit it. He claimed that there was no Occupation, that the Israeli army was in the territories solely to guard against terrorists. No Occupation, no brutality, no persecution of the Arab people. Do you believe that there is an Occupation, doctor?"

"The Israeli army is an occupying force," I said, "as a result of the continual attacks from the territories."

"And do you agree that the Jews are torturing our people?"

"The Israeli troops can be very harsh," I said. "I oppose that kind of brutality."

"And do you agree that we Palestinians have a right to defend ourselves?"

"Every people has the right to defend itself."

"Your brother refused to admit that there are Israeli war criminals, Israelis who have committed atrocities. Do you believe that, Doctor?"

"When hatred takes over, inhuman things are done," I said. "Atrocities are committed by both sides."

This answer got to Mohammed, as I knew it would.

"Spoken just like your brother," he replied. "You are denying the truth."

"Which is?"

"That the Jews drove our people out of our homes and possessed their lands. When we protested, when we fought back, they slaughtered us. And they continue to slaughter us."

Then he got up and walked out. As he did, he tossed a few words at Ahmed.

"You heard," he said. "You heard what he said. Now tell me he is not his brother."

"But he's not," Ahmed shot back. "You are not hearing him. You need to listen to what he is saying."

Mohamed did not respond. He was already gone.

Ahmed then turned to me. He must have sensed that I was upset with myself.

"You did alright, Siggie," he said. "You were not your brother and he knew it. You acknowledged the truth about the Israelis and that is bound to register with him. It's just that he is not going to give an inch. He's too angry and in too much pain to do that. But if you stick in there, you'll have a good chance to get to him."

"I don't have time for a thirty years war."

"It won't be like that, Siggie. I'll work on Mohammed. I think I can bring him around."

Barney and I didn't know what to make of Ahmed's behavior. I thought he was being sincere, that Mohammed was the stumbling block.

Barney was more skeptical, more suspicious of what he called Ahmed's clever ways.

"He's sharp," Barney said, "and very persuasive. Ahmed can make you see what he wants you to see. And he blinds you to the rest."

"Which is?"

"Keeping you at bay with one excuse after another. And trying to get you to believe this Mohammed character will soften up. That is pure deception. For a blind man like him, there is only one truth. Jews are the enemy and the only way to deal with enemies is to eliminate them. And don't forget that Ahmed is on the same team. Both have been trained as killers. They are in this together."

Barney was right—or was he? True they were on the same team, were fighting the same fight, but did that mean they were the same people? To me the two were different, fundamentally different in who they were, in the essence of themselves. But I didn't want to argue the point, and I realized that in other respects Barney was on target. Ahmed had outmaneuvered me.

"So we are nowhere?" I said. "Ahmed's managed to box me out. I've not been able to get what we need. I guess it's time to close up shop."

"Nonsense," Barney said, "we're in the game to stay. Do you drive your car without a spare tire? No way. You wouldn't do it, and neither would I. At the 23rd whatever operation we launched we always had a spare tire. If one of Barney's ideas stalls, it's time for Barney two."

Then he reached into his back pocket and withdrew a fountain pen.

"See this, Doc?" he said, it's going to write us a new start."

I said nothing. I wondered what my partner was up to.

"Looks like your routine Bar Mitzvah present, right?" he asked. "The traditional fountain pen. Also used by shrinks the world over to record the dreams and wishes that keep their patients alive. Every shrink has one. It's expected. Attracts no attention."

I was waiting for the sales pitch.

"But look here, Doctor."

He removed the pen's cap and pointed at the barrel. What do you see here? A little thickening around the middle, you say. Yes, indeed, because this pen contains a marvel of American technology. He unscrewed another part of the instrument to reveal two small batteries.

"I am proud to say this recording device was the creation of the 23rd's tech team. It's the best in the world. I can pick up the sound of someone using a toothpick at thirty feet."

I was beginning to get the picture.

"And you are presenting me with my overdue Bar Mitzvah present so I can have it handy when I'm talking with my friend, Ahmed, is that right?"

"You are a quick read, Doctor. Ahmed, Mohammed, whoever comes across your path. My guess is you'll have a lot of interesting listening ahead of you. And if you happen to be around Ahmed's girlfriend, you might want to have this little device handy. She might know things about our friend that only someone in her position would know."

At this point, I was becoming uneasy.

"You're asking me to spy on people who trust me, people I work with and care about. I can't do that. It strikes me as dirty pool."

"That's what it is, Doc. Dirty pool and necessary pool. Tough as hell, but sometimes it's the only way to nail a bad guy. On the force, I had to go undercover and wear a wire a couple of times to get evidence against some rogue cops. I hated doing it, but we had to bring these crooks down.

"Right now, we need to get what we can on Ahmed's boys. I did a check with the local FBI to see if they had anything on them and it turns out they have phone records of Mohammed and his nephew making regular calls to a known militant outfit in Pakistan. May be a red herring, but the Bureau thinks they could be planning some kind of attack on the City. We have our own case and our own reasons for needing info, but if something like this is in the works, we could be looking at a big-time disaster. So if doing a bit of dirty work can head off something like that, I'm willing to take a big gulp and swallow my scruples. But look, I understand. If this kind of thing doesn't sit right with you, I'll get back into a *schvitz* bath and see if I can come up with Barney three."

"No need," I replied. "It will be alright, just give me some time and a stiff drink. As we used to say on the addiction's unit, the superego is soluble in alcohol."

What I couldn't dissolve, though, was the question that sat like a lump in my chest.

What if I did this and we were on the wrong track, if our thinking was askew and I violated Ahmed's trust and Laura's trust for nothing, simply because we were convinced by our own wrong-headed thinking? I did not allow that thought to stay in my mind, though. I drove it underground as soon as it surfaced. I had to put aside my doubts and deal with my guilt by knowing that there was a good reason for doing what I was doing. I had to talk to myself.

Chapter 10

That wasn't so easy, however. My worry about doing something wrong and illegal worked against my ability to use the listening device. I tried a couple of times when Abdul and Mohammed were on a roll, alternatively cursing out right-wing Israeli politicians and their Arab-hating American-Jewish supporters, and throwing in praise for a couple of radical Muslim Clerics as well. Twice I slipped the pen into a shirt pocket and got into good recording position, but on both occasions my fingers cramped up and I fumbled with the switch in such an obvious—and suspicious—way, that I gave up the effort.

Meanwhile, Barney was busy polishing his undercover skills. Using the rough charm he had developed as a beat cop to handle an often-disgruntled public, he approached LaToya and managed to sell her on the idea of taking him on, a retired accounts manager for a shoe company—a position he actually held for a year before joining the NYPD—as a volunteer in the Bookkeeping Department.

He had been on the job just a few days when he called me. I was in Ahmed's office tactfully trying to fend off his suggestion that I offer my services to the Home Visits Department.

Barney's voice came through in a half-whisper.

"Got to be quick," he said, "but I have news. Ahmed's boys have been skimming cream right off the top of the milk bottle. They've been filching money from the pool of donations and grant funds that come into this place."

"You've caught them at it?"

"Not exactly. I came across a stack of invoices from what I'm sure are dummy companies that bill and get paid for supplies that don't exist."

"And these guys can get away with that?"

"Don't seem to have much trouble pulling it off. One of their crew must have gone to forgery school. Whoever he is, he does a pretty decent job. It's not easy to spot this stuff as phony."

"But Lenny did."

"He did and that was his undoing. Probably found discrepancies in the books and then uncovered the fraud. But then he must have slipped up, left notes or papers out in the open when he went to the john or something and one of the Muslims came in and caught him out. Once they realized he knew, he was a dead man."

As Barney was speaking, a memory of Lenny, dear Lenny the absent-minded professor, rose from within. And with it a searing pain that ripped at my insides.

"But these *momsas* are not going to get away with what they've done," Barney was saying, as though he sensed and was trying to ease my pain. I said nothing, but in my mind I thanked my partner for reaching out.

"What did they do, pocket the money?" I asked.

"Don't think so. My guess is they use it to fund their operations. The FBI boys suspect we're dealing with a terrorist cell that's looking to hit targets in the City. The Bureau is looking to us to pass on any info we can pick up.

"But these *gonifs* are also into something else. I found copies of a lease for office space in a nearby building and orders for books and pamphlets on the Muslim religion, together with a dozen copies of the Qur'an."

"Sounds like somebody wants to start a Sunday School."

"Sunday School Jihadist-style. These shysters are looking to make converts. My guess is they will aim for the most vulnerable kids, the troubled ones who are dirt poor, have nothing, and carry around deep resentment for whites and white society. They are easy targets for brain-washing and recruitment to the cause."

"And they are planning to do this right under LaToya's nose?"

"LaToya won't be a problem, not if Ahmed works on her. She is totally bewitched by him, thinks he is the smartest man on the planet. Ahmed could set up a prayer room at the Center, promote the idea that praying to Allah is the best treatment for dyslexia, and LaToya would have half the kids in the place lining up for the cure."

Barney had barely finished this sentence when his voice shifted into a half whisper, "Got to hang up. They are coming in."

"Be careful," I called into the phone, "watch yourself." But it was too late, the line was dead. I hung up. I did not want to think of what could have happened.

For some time I puzzled over what Barney said. If it was true that the Arabs were into conversion, what was Ahmed's role in this? Had he initiated the program? Was it okay with him to sell total devotion to Allah and the idea that the greatest glory is to give one's life for the Faith? Had he come that far?

I had no answer to that question, or even clear proof that religious instruction of any kind was underway. But then, a few weeks later, confirmation came from a surprising source.

It arrived in the form of a phone call from Laura.

"Bill, I'm worried about Marco," she said.

"What's going on Laura?"

"He's acting like some kind of Muslim zealot. Praising Allah, quoting from the Qur'an, the whole bit."

"How long has this been going on?"

"It's been a few weeks. Since he's been in a religious education program."

"Started by Ahmed?"

"Actually Mohammed is in charge. The idea is to teach kids about the world's religions."

"All of them?"

"Supposedly. Right now it's all about Muslim beliefs. But as far as I can see, what they're doing is over the top. More indoctrination than teaching. I was worried about this kind of thing with Lenny. I didn't want my kid turned Orthodox, with all its rigidities, but this is worse. A vulnerable kid like Marco can get into trouble. He could be persuaded to do dangerous things."

"Have you spoken to Ahmed about this?"

"I mentioned it, but for some reason he didn't want to get into the whole thing. He simply said Mohammed is a responsible person. That may be, but I don't like what I see."

Laura asked if I could look into the matter and let her know what I'd learned.

I said I would, that I wanted to do whatever I could for Marco.

"My brother loved your son." I said. "He wanted him to get well and be strong. I'll do all I can for the boy—and for Lenny. I have a partner who knows how to investigate situations like this," I added. "We'll find out what is going on. But first I'm going to ask Ahmed about it. I'll be interested in what he says."

When I approached Ahmed, his response was brief and straightforward.

"We teach religious faith as an important part of life," he said. "No matter what a child's religion, he needs to know about it, know its history and origins."

"No emphasis on the Muslim religion?"

"It's what we start with. It's what we know best. We want the children to understand what it really is, without the distortions they are bound to hear."

"And you teach other religions?"

"That's our plan. We aim to get to them all."

That was it, plain and simple. Spoken matter-of-factly so I would take him at his word.

Chapter 11

When I reported that conversation to Barney and also what Laura had told me about Marco, he responded with a plan of action.

"We'll pay the place an after-hours visit," he announced. "Our FBI friends take a keen interest in educational opportunities like this."

"And just how are we supposed to get in there?"

"Just leave it to me, Doc. When it comes to break-ins, I've got world class help."

"From who, Willie Sutton?"

"Someone who taught Willie all he knew, told him if he wanted a big payday, he needed to go where the money was. My man, Leon, is the best. Show him any lock made in the US of A, and he'll have it opened in under two minutes. He'd be sitting on a fortune today, but he always managed to trip himself up. He needed your couch, Doc. He'd make dumb mistakes and we'd catch up with him. Finally quit the game and has gone legit as the best ex-con locksmith in the business. We've become friendly and once in a while he'll do a job for me. I'll call him and arrange our visit for midnight. That's when Leon's fingers work best."

"What if we're spotted? From what I hear, Mohammed and friends run a restricted operation. They don't admit Jews to their school."

"Well then we'll break down that barrier. The UJA will name us Jewish pioneers of the year."

"That's great, Barney, but breaking and entering is not in my skill set. I can barely operate my bedside clock, no less pull off something like this. I'm sure to trip on a lamp wire or something and get us caught."

"Not to worry, Doc. Leon and I will take care of everything. You just watch and learn. You'll get the hang of it real quick. Next time you'll be the first one in the door."

"Thanks for the vote of confidence, but I'm just fine bringing up the rear. But, seriously, Barney, what happens if things go wrong and we get caught?"

"We won't, Doc. I'll have a squad car from the precinct sitting out front. If one of their boys shows up, our guys will give us a heads up and we'll be out of there in plenty of time."

"Okay, but if things go wrong and we get caught and end up on Isis reality TV as stars of the guillotine hour, I'm holding you responsible."

Barney made the arrangements, and at the stroke of twelve we slipped into the old factory building in which Mohammed had rented space. Leon was waiting at the entrance of Suite 402, on whose glass fronted door appeared the simple designation; Religious Studies Department.

Leon was a slight, wiry fellow who weighed in at no more than a hundred thirty pounds, wore ankle high sneakers, and sported a Knick's t-shirt which bore the uniform number of Carmelo Anthony, his personal hero.

Leon insisted on shaking hands all around, then proceeded to pick the front door lock, as advertised, in just under two minutes. Inside, were a half dozen folding chairs, a like number of public school-type desks that looked to be remnants from the last century, and a long table that appeared to have been retrieved from a pile of cast-off furniture. On each chair was a copy of the Qur'an and on the table a stack of pamphlets that referred to Israel as the new Third Reich and America as a Jewish fortress that sent death squads to Arab countries. There was more, too; leaflets calling for the destruction of Israel, all-out war on the Zionist conspiracy, and relentless attacks on the imperialist countries that supported Israel.

One leaflet offered a unique approach to anti-Semitism, one that I had not encountered before. I was intrigued by its title, "One Hundred Lies in the Jewish Bible." I wondered how the selection was made and I was tempted to filch it for bedtime reading. We took half a dozen pictures and were out of there in only slightly longer than the five minutes that Barney had predicted.

"We got good stuff," he said. "I'll get the photos sent around to the Bureau and it will keep an eye on this place in case the folks here decide to add a Jihadist practicum to the curriculum."

We had just left and were in the hallway when Barney's phone went off. It was one of the cops in the patrol car on the street. Barney held the phone out so I could hear.

"A black van is parked across the street," a crackling voice came through. "He's circled the block a couple of times. Could be trouble. Suggest you exit through the rear door. We'll cover the front."

Barney acknowledged the call, then motioned for us to follow him. The three of us, Barney leading the way, headed for a nearby staircase, walked single file down four flights of concrete stairs and out a creaky, thickly-rusted, rear door. Then, keeping our formation, we hugged the building wall, crept around to the front, and made a dash for Barney's car.

Once inside, I scanned the street. I could see no black van, no vehicle of any kind. When we started moving, though, and had reached the first intersection, I spotted a van parked on a side street about half a block away. Its headlights were on and its motor was idling. I watched through the rear window. As soon as we passed the intersection, the car turned into the main road and fell into line behind us. I alerted Barney who muttered something that sounded like a Yiddish curse word. Then, saying nothing more, he sped up, made a series of sharp angle turns, and headed down a narrow alleyway that ran alongside Schlossman's, his favorite delicatessen.

"I think we're okay for the moment," Barney said, "Arabs don't like Deli."

I checked the roadway behind us. It was empty. Barney had managed to lose our pursuers. "They'll be back," he announced. "These fellows are pros. They are not going home, you can bet on that."

Barney was right. When he dropped me off a half block from my house—I live on a dead-end street that is hard to maneuver out of—I noticed what looked like a large vehicle sitting in the dark not fifty yards away. I had not traveled more than ten, fifteen yards down the road when I heard the sound of an engine starting up, then being gunned. I turned and saw the silver grill of the van coming straight for me. Out of pure instinct, I leaped onto the sidewalk as it hurtled past like a giant artillery shell. It missed killing me by matter of inches.

Then nausea took hold, along with a profound dizziness, and I dropped to my knees and retched vomit and bile onto the grass that bordered the sidewalk leading to my house. I slipped to the ground and sat with my head beneath my knees. I remained that way for a good ten minutes, suddenly so weak that I felt it impossible to get to my feet. A cruising police car stopped on the road, and from the passenger side a cop leaned out the window and asked if I was all right. I nodded and waved, and the police drove on, leaving me with the kindly advise to go home, get some sleep, and watch my wallet on the way.

It took some time for me to do that. When I felt able to start for home, I could only move slowly, taking small, careful steps like a feeble person. It took me a good five minutes to cover the hundred yards to my front door.

When I managed to reach my second-floor bedroom, I threw myself onto the bed, creating enough of a disturbance to rouse my wife from sleep. In a foggy voice she asked where I had been, but was too drowsy to question me when I muttered something about being out with a few people from the Center.

Early the next morning I called Barney. He had driven away after dropping me off and had not witnessed the attempt on my life. When I told him what happened, he was alarmed. It was the first time that I had heard a note of fear in his voice.

"They have us on the Lenny list," he said. "We are going to have to move fast. We need to get whatever evidence we can, turn it over to Steiner, and pack it in. At this point I'm ready for sunny Florida and Assisted Living. Any Jihadists I run into from now on are going to be in my dreams." Barney then outlined our next move. He would return to the hotel, survey the staff, and see if he could turn up anyone who had seen Ahmed in the time frame that the coroner had established for Lenny's death. Barney promised to meet me at my office once he'd checked things out at the hotel. Then we would exchange information and go from there.

What, at that point, I couldn't get out of my head was the question that had dogged me all along but that now took on a pressing—and torturing—quality.

How much exactly was Ahmed involved in all that happened? Twice vans had barely missed smashing into me. The last time clearly an attempt at execution. Was Ahmed behind these attempts? Was he intent on eliminating me as he had eliminated my brother? My wife was certain that he was. For her there was no doubt about it. Lenny had posed a danger to Ahmed and as a result he was strung up in a hotel bathroom. As another Strickman who threatened Ahmed and his mission. I, too, was targeted for elimination.

Alice was convincing. I accepted the fact that she was seeing things more clearly than I, but it took a personal injury, Ahmed turning against me, for me finally, to rid myself of the uncertainty that had plagued me from the beginning, the nagging question as to whether we had it right about Ahmed. And to see what now was evident; that he no longer endorsed the values we had shared, that he had adopted the Jihadist view of the world with its skewed vision, its distortion of reality, its distain for the truth.

Chapter 12

It happened as a revenge attack in the warfare between Arab and Jew, the one that was playing out on the streets of New York.

This time it was the Jews who struck. A retaliation for the gunning down of children at a Jewish school by an Islamic terrorist. Two youths from the Hasidic community drove an SUV into a group of Arab boys playing Capture the Flag on a Manhattan side street.

One of the boys was hit in the flank and thrown ten feet in the air. He died instantly. Two others suffered multiple injuries and were transported to our hospital in a private car belonging to the father of one of the victims.

When I arrived, Ahmed was examining one of the injured boys in the ER. The parents of the dead child were sitting alone in a hallway, almost motionless. Their son's body had been transported to the morgue. The parents had been told to sit and wait, that someone from Social Services would come to speak with them. Thus far no one had appeared. I took in the scene from a spot in the ER and observed Ahmed. For some time, he did not notice me. He was concentrating on his exam, carefully checking a young boy's respirations, palpating the abdomen, and inspecting the extremities. All the while he was dictating his findings to an intern who was taking down everything he said.

When the examination was complete and the child was being transferred to a gurney for transport to an OR, Ahmed looked up and saw me. He nodded, but said nothing. His face registered anguish. As he turned to summon the next patient, a nurse approached him, pointed to the couple sitting in the hallway, and whispered something. Ahmed nodded and beckoned to me. He took me aside, explained that these were the parents of the boy who had been killed, and asked if I would go to them and do what I could to be of comfort.

I murmured a word of assent and approached the couple. I introduced myself, expressed my condolences at their loss, and asked if I might sit with them. For some time I did just that, sat alongside them, a silent presence, just someone who was with them in their grief. It was the father who at last broke the silence.

"Why such hatred?" He asked. "Why kill an innocent child?"

At this the mother wept.

"It's a horror," is all I could say. "Totally senseless."

I took the hands of both parents and held them in my own.

We sat that way for several minutes and gradually the mother began to speak, to tell me about her son and what a fine boy he was.

"A musician who played the clarinet and a soccer player, too," she said. The father joined in with additional comments about the boy's talents. He was in the midst of relating another of his son's accomplishments when the door to the hallway swung open and three figures approached; Mohammed, Abdul, and a third man, who I did not recognize.

Mohammed spoke first, and bluntly. "Thank you for sitting with these people, Dr. Strickman," he said, "but you will not be needed here anymore. Actually, Dr. Aslam should not have sent you here. These are not your people. You don't know their ways. We have brought a psychiatrist from their community who will look after them." He gestured toward the third man who, in response, nodded to me.

"Dr. Abbodi knows their traditions, and what to do in a situation like this," Mohammed added.

The parents looked befuddled. The mother reached out and touched my arm,

"This doctor has been very nice, very comforting," she said.

"I'm sure," Mohammed replied, "but he's not appropriate for this situation. Dr. Abbodi will be of great help to you" Mohammed looked at me.

Cold fury took hold of me then, and a barely controllable urge to scream at Mohammed and ask what the hell he thought he was doing and to get the hell out of here before he got carried out.

Abdul must have sensed my rage. He took a step forward, as though to protect Mohammed. He glowered at me, conveying a clear warning. I managed to control myself so that I responded only by barking, "we'll see about this." Then I turned and marched off in search of Ahmed. I found him talking with a surgeon who had just come down from the OR after operating on a badly wounded child.

I waited half a minute or so, then blurted out that I had to talk to Dr. Aslam on an urgent matter. Taking Ahmed aside, I explained, now with unconcealed anger, what had just happened. Ahmed listened, then told me to wait there. He went to find Mohammed. After a minute or so I heard the sound of arguing and raised voices coming from the hallway. Then, red-faced and clearly agitated, Ahmed reappeared. He looked at me, and shook his head. "The man is impossible, Siggie," he said. "He is in one of his states. There is no reasoning with him. He doesn't want you in there. Says there is no place for a Jew in this situation. He'll start a fight if you go back in there; he'll raise hell. There is no point in it, Siggie. When he's this way, you just have to stay away. I've seen him like this before. He can get violent. It's best to let it go, Sig. Don't get involved. Somebody will get hurt."

"In other words, you are going to let him get away with this, barging in and disrupting what I was trying to do with these people. This is totally destructive. He doesn't give a damn about them. The guy is a vicious anti-Semite. And you are doing nothing about it."

"I understand, Siggie, I do, but you've got to listen to me. I've seen Mohammed like this. He can be dangerous."

"How is it you are always protecting Mohammed?" I asked. "Poor Mohammed. He loses his temper, he threatens, he can be dangerous, so we all have to cow-tow to him. Well do you know something? I've had enough of Mr. Mohammed, more than enough of that bigot. As far as I'm concerned, the guy is a Fascist bully. You can take him and that creep, Abdul, and shove them up your ass."

And I walked out. I was fuming, and to try to calm myself I walked around the block before I headed upstairs to the psychiatric floor. Then I used my cell phone to call Barney. He didn't answer but I let go and screamed into the phone. "This is the second time he's sided with that fascist, Mohammed," I shouted at the answering machine.

'All the time with the excuses, the making nice. Well, fuck them both. They are two of a kind, Jew haters plain and simple. I've been a damn fool to think anything else.'

I hung up, feeling momentarily purged. And then I recognized that the time had come to take action. No more doubts and hesitancy; no more timidity masquerading as ethics, as honorable behavior. These people were our enemies. They were out to kill us. And unless we stopped them, no doubt they would kill many more.

I would adhere to Barney's strategy and use the pen he had given me to record conversations with Ahmed and Mohammed in the hope that in an unguarded moment they would reveal themselves to be who they were; terrorists bent on launching an attack on the City. And with luck I might catch Ahmed in a compromising statement about Lenny's death.

This whole scheme, I realized, would be a dangerous undertaking. If the Muslims discovered what I was up to, I'd be in the same place Lenny was when he came across their dummy company scheme.

This operation would take planning, skill, and a lot of *Sechel*. By that measure I was not at all sure that I was qualified for the job. But there was no choice. We needed more evidence about the intentions of these people, and Barney was counting on me to obtain it. And as a designated undercover agent and honorary member of the 23rd's distinguished detective squad, I had to try.

Chapter 13

The first thing I did when I returned to the Center—and it nearly killed me to do so—was to seek out Mohammed and say that I was sorry for the unpleasantness at the hospital and that he was right to say that a psychiatrist of their faith would be in a better position to comfort the grieving parents.

He simply nodded in agreement, then uttered the kind of comment I anticipated. "A Jew killed their child," he said, "No Jew could comfort them."

I did not argue. I held back from giving voice to what I was thinking; that what Mohammed said was pure projection. He, an Arab, would never comfort Jewish parents of a child killed by the Arab gunman. But I kept my mouth shut. I was trying, with difficulty, to implement my strategy.

I had to wait for the right time to initiate the charged political discussions that might produce the kind of self-indicting comments I was seeking.

It came as the result of some terrible news from the West Bank. A week earlier two Israeli teenagers had gone missing. Three days later their bodies were found in a ditch about a mile from their homes. They had been murdered by a gang of angry Palestinian youths who were enraged by the arrest for stone-throwing of one of their group.

About a week after that, the charred body of a Palestinian teenager was found on the bank of a river. The boy had been abducted and tortured, then strangled to death. His body had been set on fire by a band of settlers as revenge for the prior killings.

I was horrified and depressed by this news. It seemed to me to epitomize a rapidly deteriorating situation; one that was plunging the region into another brutal and tragic war.

The barbaric murders were the talk of the Center staff and I had no doubt that my Arab friends would have much to say about them.

When the opportunity came and Mohammed walked into Ahmed's office while I was talking with him, I reached into my pocket, flipped on the recording device, and initiated the discussion with a casual observation.

"Terrible situation in Israel right now." I threw out to no one in particular, "It could lead to another Intifada."

Mohammed's reply was immediate.

"And it will," he said, "you can be sure of that. Our people will take to the streets. We will let these barbarians know that they will pay with their blood. These so-called settlers have become monsters."

"Something like this was inevitable once children of theirs were murdered." I said, I was trying to stir up some fire.

Mohammed looked at me with disgust.

"And how many thousands of Arab lives have been lost before that happened, Doctor?" he asked, "how much suffering has been imposed by these people, intruders who have stolen our land and have persecuted our people for protesting?

"That land was part of Judea, the land of the ancient Hebrews, long before your people got there," I said. "The idea that this is Arab territory is nothing but a myth."

This was the position maintained by religious Jews, one that I myself questioned, but I knew it would enrage Mohammed. It did.

"You are lying through your teeth," he shouted, "trying to use the Bible to justify the thievery and murder committed by your people. That is the Strickman way, Lenny's way. Poison the minds of our kids with one lie after another. Don't think you will get away with that kind of behavior, Doctor."

"I have no doubt about that," I replied. "You made sure that my brother was silenced. Talk about violence. You so-called peaceable Muslims certainly know a lot about that."

I had managed to stir fire under Mohammed who was rapidly losing his temper and I hoped to do the same to Ahmed. When he jumped in, though, it was to maintain that the Muslim religion does not endorse violence, that his people resort to it only when they are forced to strike back, to fight for their lives.

"Is that why you joined militants who slaughter innocent people?"

"For three decades I watched my family and my people defiled and humiliated, Siggie," he said. "It took me a long time, but I finally realized that the only way to combat what was being done to us was to rise up, fight fire with fire."

He had all but confessed that he had allied himself with Jihadists. He even justified murder.

"There is no question of killing for its own sake," he added. "It is a matter of doing what has to be done to obtain our freedom. We have no wish to kill innocent people, but that is inevitable in war, it's the price both sides have to pay."

I had pretty much what I wanted. Barney would be pleased, and with this tape and the eye witness account of Ahmed being in Lenny's hotel room prior to his being murdered, it was likely that Steiner could reopen the case.

Laura and Marco, however, could easily be swept up in all that was happening. With the indoctrination of children that was being carried out under the guise of religious instruction, these Arabs could very well persuade Marco that the glory of Heaven awaited if he did Allah's bidding and became a suicide bomber. And with the inside information that Laura had about Ahmed, she could be in danger on two fronts; if Steiner pursued an investigation, he could charge her as an accessory to murder, and with what she knew about Ahmed, the Arabs might view her as a threat to them.

I had come to care deeply about Laura and her child. Marco was the son Lenny never had, and I wanted to honor his memory in a way that I knew would have meant a great deal to him; by caring for and protecting the boy.

I realized I needed to get over to Laura's place and alert her to what I now knew. But I also understood that what I had to say would likely fall on deaf ears. Laura was Ahmed's lover. She would be in his corner. It would be very hard for her to hear what I had to say.

But I had the tape. My hope was that hearing what was on it would reach her in a way that I could not. Once Laura had listened to it, she could no longer deny the truth. Tapes don't lie.

Chapter 14

As soon as I reached Laura's place and we'd had a chance to exchange greetings, I came to the point.

"I want to talk with you about something, Laura." I began, "I've been meaning to for some time."

Laura looked at me. There was an expression of unease, of apprehension, on her face, as though she feared I'd come as the bearer of bad news.

"It's about Ahmed," I said. "Ahmed and Mohammed and the Muslims at the Center."

She waited and said nothing.

"I'm not sure that you really know who they are."

Laura looked at me as though I had gone bonkers.

"I know this sounds odd," I said, "I mean, since you know Ahmed very well." I almost said intimately, but caught myself. "But I'm not sure that he has told you everything about himself."

"Actually, I think I know him very well."

"You do. Of course you do. Please don't take this the wrong way, but there are some things Ahmed may not have felt comfortable revealing."

"And you know what these are?"

I nodded and then proceeded to relate what I was not sure she knew; Ahmed's mysterious disappearance, his joining a militant outfit—I now had his acknowledgement of this on record—and my own strong suspicion that he and his Muslim friends were part of an Isis cell that was planning to carry out attacks on targets in New York City. I wasn't going to tell her about the murder—to be told that her lover was a cold-blooded killer would deliver a shock that was bound to be traumatic—but I got carried away and added that, too.

Laura had been listening quietly, skeptically, I thought, but when I spoke of murder, she reacted.

"That is ridiculous," she said. "Where did you get this idiocy? That is the craziest thing I've ever heard. Ahmed is one of the sweetest people I know. He and Mohammed both. They have been nothing but good to Marco. Absolutely devoted, and great to me, too."

"I don't doubt it. People have many faces, Laura. They have shown you only one; and that face is also a mask," I added.

"Bill, I have to tell you, you sound truly mad. Have you been drinking? Either that or you have OD'd on TV crime shows."

"Actually, neither," I said. "And I'm not any crazier than usual. I wasn't intending to tell you any of this. I figured sooner or later you'd find out for yourself and then you wouldn't have to take my word for it. You'd be convinced. But then I realized that would be dangerous. These people could turn on you, Laura. If somehow you crossed them or they thought you knew too much and were going to expose them, you'd be in real danger. They have no compunction about killing. They've killed already. None of us are safe."

"I hear you, Bill, but frankly I'm having trouble believing any of this. Do you have any proof of what you are saying?"

At that point, I reached into my pocket and extracted the pen recorder.

"It's all here," I said, "everything."

I held up the pen for Laura to see. "All recorded on this little device."

"What is?"

"A conversation I've just had with Ahmed and Mohammed. Who they really are comes through. They hate Israel and want to drive it into the sea. Hate it and its people with a passion. And they hate America, too. Any ally of Israel's is their enemy. As far as they are concerned, if we are hit with another 9-11 tomorrow, it will not be too soon."

"And you say you have all of this recorded?"

"Right here." I extended the pen to her. She did not take it.

"And when did you record this conversation?"

"Today. Earlier today. We had a three-way conversation, Ahmed, Mohammed and me."

"Did they know that you were recording them?"

"If they had known that, I wouldn't have heard what I did. They would have covered up completely."

"But that was dishonest, Bill. Recording people without their consent is not only deceitful, it is unlawful."

"Look, we can't worry about niceties of morality in a situation like this. You don't seem to understand how dangerous these people are. They would be on the verge of carrying out an attack that could kill hundreds of people. Once you've heard the tape, you'll understand."

"I can't do it, Bill. If I agree to listen, I'd be giving my approval for a crime."

I could see what I was up against. She wasn't going to yield. She didn't want to know.

"All right, then," I said, "I understand. But I want you to do something."

"What is that?"

Laura had mentioned that she was expecting Ahmed and Mohammed momentarily, that they were coming over to work with Marco; Ahmed to do some physical training with him and Mohammed to act as a tutor in language skills and math. Abdul would be arriving a bit later to help out where he could.

"Before they get started with Marco, I want you to bring them into this living room, sit them down, and ask them some hard questions. Make them talk about themselves and their philosophy, what they believe, who they are, and what groups in their home countries they are connected with. Satisfy yourself that I have not been exaggerating."

"What makes you think they will tell me the truth?"

"They will if you make clear that you are on their side, that you are sympathetic to the Palestinians and their cause, which, in fact, you told me you were. If they believe you to be a true ally, they will be very interested in recruiting you to their team. And if for any reason they won't talk, you can always withhold permission for them to have further contact with Marco or yourself until you know exactly who they are and what they stand for. If you hold the line, they will come through."

"I'm not sure I can be that firm."

"This is important, Laura."

"All right. I'll try."

"And let me know what you've learned. We'll need to make some plans to ensure your safety in case they should decide later that you know too much."

"Don't be so dramatic, Bill. I will be perfectly safe."

"I hope you're right."

I knew from what Laura had said about using a hidden recorder, her indignation at the very idea of it, that she would not consent to my using the pen in this situation. And for her to announce that she wished to record her conversation with the visitors would defeat our purpose. But I wanted to have a record of that conversation as well as the one I already had. I thought it possible that in Laura's presence, a sympathetic woman, one or the other of them might talk more freely and I could obtain some truly incriminating material.

I asked Laura for a glass of water, and while she was out of the room, I removed the recorder-pen from my breast pocket and placed it carefully behind a large table lamp that stood a foot or so from the living room couch. Resting inconspicuously behind and at the base of the lamp, an Oriental-type, it was well out of sight. According to Barney, the range of the device was such that it could easily record a conversation taking place anywhere in that room or in the adjacent dining room.

My plan was to say nothing to Laura—I well knew what her reaction would be—take my leave, find a place to conceal myself across the street, and wait for Ahmed and Mohammed to arrive. When, through a window, I spotted them seated in the living room, I would activate the recording devise remotely, using my cell phone in the way that Barney had demonstrated. The next day I would retrieve the pen from its hiding place. I would find a reason to come by Laura's place again, perhaps to discuss what she had learned and what we were going to do about it. And while there I would stroll into the living room, and when Laura was not looking, slip the pen into my pocket. Thus, with a bit of *Maazel*, Barney and I might have what we needed.

When the job was done and the machine activated, I left my hiding place and walked a couple of blocks before catching a bus home. On the way, I kept thinking about Lenny and what a good man he was and what these Muslims did to him. A searing pain ripped through me at the thought that he was forever gone, that I would never see him again. Then cold fury took hold of me and I found myself making a vow, the kind of pledge I could never have conceived of making. I vowed vengeance.

Chapter 15

After I left Laura's place, I headed for my office. I had several patients to see that afternoon, but before I got started I had arranged to spend a few minutes with Barney. He was to report on his latest scouting trip to the Pearl Hotel. He had gone there in search of another witness. If he could find someone else, perhaps another hotel employee, who had seen Ahmed entering or exiting Lenny's room prior to the time of the murder, that would pretty much cinch the case. Then Steiner would re-open the investigation.

He was late arriving, and when he showed up he was disoriented, as though he'd fallen and struck his head on the way over.

On entering my office he sat heavily on my couch and for a long minute remained silent. Then he seemed to search my face before speaking. Finally he began.

"When you signed me up for this job," he said, "I told you you were resurrecting a dinosaur, right?"

"Something like that."

"But I didn't tell you that the one you picked out has a brain the size of an amoeba, did I?"

"That big? You never mentioned that. Lucky, I got the bonus size. I knew when I chose you that was my lucky day."

"I have a hunch that you are going to change your tune very shortly, Doctor, in fact, in the next thirty seconds."

"What's wrong?" I asked.

"Not much. Just that we have a small job ahead of us. We have to find our missing case. It's vanished."

"What are you talking about?"

"We may have been looking in the wrong pew, my friend. There's a very good chance that Ahmed didn't do it."

His hair was all askew and he looked like he was coming apart. Whatever was troubling him was doing a job on his kishkes.

I waited.

"I was at the hotel, Doc," he said, "talking to the staff, looking for another witness, when I got a call. This surprised me. I wasn't expecting to hear from anyone. It turns out it's a buddy of mine from the local precinct. He's got something that will interest me, he says. His men picked up our hooker for shoplifting. The kid was trying to walk out of Staples with one of those fancy new cell phones in his backpack. They brought him in and started to book him, but before they did, the kid announces he wants to make a deal. If my friend will forget about today's caper, he'll give him information about the Lenny case."

"What kind of information?"

"The kid won't say. He's playing it cool. But he hints he's got something we'd like to know."

"Something he hasn't already told us?"

"Apparently. Well, anyway my buddy asks me to come over to the precinct. They figure I knew the kid and maybe I can figure out if he really has something or if he's bluffing."

"How did your friend know to call you, or that you've had anything to do with our boy?"

"I've been filling him in on the case, keeping him up to date. He's a real vet, been at the precinct over thirty years. Knows everyone in the neighborhood and is sharp at picking up the buzz from the street. I figured if he knew what was going on in our case, he'd be in a position to pass on any info that might come his way."

"So what happened?"

"I went over there and I put the kid on the hot seat, pressured him to admit he was trying to pull a fast one, that he had nothing we didn't already know. But I came away thinking the kid has been holding something back, keeping an ace up his sleeve in case he got into a jam and needed to play it."

"So you got your friend to make the deal?"

"That wasn't easy. He didn't trust our boy, thought he was pulling a number on us. But he finally went along with me."

"And?"

"And the hooker hits me with a bombshell. He tells me he spoke to Lenny a good half hour after Ahmed left the hotel. Spoke to him on his cell phone. Claims he was out in front of the hotel looking for a mark on the night before the murder when he sees Ahmed come out and get into a cab."

"He knew for sure it was Ahmed?"

"I grilled him on that. Made him give me a description, head to toe. It was Ahmed all right. Either that or he has an identical twin. Anyway, the kid claimed that about thirty minutes later Lenny calls from his room to cancel their appointment for the following week. Didn't give much of an explanation, just that he won't be able to make it, his plans have changed and he won't be in the neighborhood."

"And you're sure this actually happened, that the kid wasn't pulling a fast one?"

"I don't think so. I quizzed him pretty thoroughly. His story was consistent. It seemed to hold up."

"But how did he know we'd want that piece of information?"

"The boy may be a hooker, but he's got smarts. We'd questioned him several times about the man he'd seen in the lobby, the dark-skinned fellow. He put two and two together and figured the guy was probably a suspect and that we would be very interested in his comings and goings; when he was in the hotel and when he left. The kid figured he had info that we'd want and that he had himself a bargaining chip that he could use the next time the cops picked him up for soliciting or loitering, or whatever they decided to charge him with to get him off the streets."

"So that's it? Ahmed is not our man. He didn't kill my brother? We bloodhounds have spent weeks barking up the wrong tree? Is that our situation?"

"Looks that way, Doc. I came away from grilling the kid almost convinced that he was telling us the truth."

"Almost?"

"Well as I said, the kid is clever, but I kept wondering to myself is he that clever? Or are we falling into a trap set by someone who is out of his league, someone who is playing us for fools, who knows how to manipulate the boy to get us off his back."

"You think Ahmed put him up to this?"

"It's possible. Ahmed must have known about Lenny's being gay, or if he didn't, hanging around that hotel would have made it obvious. The place is a pick-up joint for old guys and their studs. Besides, a couple of bucks put into the right hands would have given Ahmed all the information he needed, including the fact that Lenny had a steady date with our boy. And it would have been no problem for him to locate the kid—he hangs around the hotel all the time—and pay him off to feed us the yarn about getting a call from Lenny after he saw Ahmed leave the hotel."

"And that would give Ahmed the perfect alibi. Talk about clever."

"If that's what happened. That's the rub, Doc. We don't know if I'm on the money or talking two-bit theory."

"I'm putting my money on you, Barney. But how are we going to know?"

We need to go back to square one, Doc, start over."

"Meaning what?"

"When I got bumped up to detective, I had an old-timer for a supervisor, a real *altacocker,* and cranky as hell. But the guy knew a thing or two and he taught me something important. 'When you are on a murder one case,' he would say,' and you hit a wall, you need to return to go and start over. You need to take another look at everything you've been over a dozen times, every thread, every scrap of paper you can find. That's when you are liable to see something new, something that's been in front of your nose all along and you never saw it. Or you saw it and passed it over; simply passed it by as of no account.'"

"So what am I supposed to do, use a magnifying glass on Lenny's shorts?"

"If necessary, yes. We need to go back to the drawing board and examine everything that belonged to Lenny, everything he owned, including his collection of Jockey shorts."

"We've done that already, Barney. Alice and I cleaned out Lenny's apartment and whatever he had in his hotel room and went over pretty much everything. The whole kit and kaboodle is stored in our attic. Alice is the thorough type. She made a master list of everything Lenny owned. We went through the whole lot and I can tell you there is nothing there, nothing that is remotely useful. If we are looking for a clue as to who wrapped a fucking lamp cord around my brother's neck, we are not going to find it in his underwear drawer.

"Maybe not. Maybe you'll find it in the toe of one of his socks, a scrap of paper with the name of his killer scrawled on it, tucked in there because Lenny figured that as a shrink you would know that compulsives hide things in their socks."

I looked at Barney. He seemed totally mad. I figured the disappointment we'd had and all the aggravation with the case had gotten to him.

"Fine," I said. "We'll go back to "go" and I'll make sure to inspect every pair of socks, and every pair of Jockey shorts, including the waistband. Lenny might have scribbled the killer's name on it so I would find it when I sorted out his shorts."

Barney reached over and touched me on the arm.

"Good thinking, Doc." He said. "That's the kind of police work that's going to pay off for us."

"I'm learning," I said. But my mind was elsewhere. I was trying to recall the 800 number for a company that advertised on the radio, an outfit that helps find Assisted Living places for the elderly. The number came back to me and I made a note to myself to make the call, get the necessary information, and present it to Barney when he returned from his next wild goose chase.

Chapter 16

After Barney left and I was alone and able to think about what he had told me, I was ready to throw in the towel. Our all-thumbs investigation had gone nowhere. We were back at square one and I was ready to declare my adventure in the gumshoe trade a washout and return to the comparatively simple job of being a shrink.

I told Alice what had happened and she did her best to commiserate with me. In addition, she showed admirable restraint by holding back what I suspected she was thinking; that instead of taking ourselves seriously as detectives, Barney and I ought to do our thing on The Comedy Hour as we had a shot at making it big as the next Odd Couple.

It didn't help to have a *meshuga* partner who suddenly had become an obsessional lunatic, possessed by the fantasy that if we examined every object Lenny touched from his skull cap to his orthopedic shoes, especially made to raise his fallen arches, we would come up with some valuable discovery. No doubt in Barney's mind this would be the clue that would break open the case and show up the professionals like Steiner, who then would have to acknowledge our Sherlock-like ingenuity.

I had no interest in trudging up to the attic, sitting in a closed and musty space for several hours, and undertaking the fruitless task of picking apart books, papers and articles of clothing, each one of which evoked memories of my brother and different—often quite idiosyncratic—features of his personality. This I knew would be a painful process and a useless one.

I could not refuse Barney, though. To do so would be to end not only our investigation—no great loss there—but our partnership. I had become used to the guy, crazy as he was, in the way that, over the years, I had become used to my brother. For reasons totally opaque to me, I could not imagine not having Barney at my side; Barney with his bloodhound nose that took us in all the wrong directions.

So I made my way up to the attic—it required climbing an old and decidedly unstable flight of stairs—and flung myself into an ancient leather recliner, torn in half a dozen places, that for strictly neurotic reasons we continued to transport from one dwelling to the next.

When we cleaned out Lenny's apartment, Alice and I did a quick survey of the bachelor miscellany that filled it, declared the furnishings to be a collection of Salvation Army rejects, and leaving those elephantine pieces behind, stuffed Lenny's belongings into three suitcases which we loaded into the trunk of our car.

When we reached home, we got our son to help us—he objected quite vigorously to being called away from the latest and most violent video game yet—and between us we managed to carry and drag the valises, as Lenny always called them, up three floors and into the large, dusty space that was our attic. I had done pretty much the same thing, although much more easily, with the possessions that I retrieved from Lenny's hotel room. Among these was a book I had lent him. It had been a gift for my birthday, which he had helped celebrate at our house just a month before he died. The book, a modern history of Israel by the noted journalist, Avi Shavit, had been given to me by a friend who praised it as a fair-minded and evenly-balanced assessment of Israel's strengths and weaknesses. I, too, was impressed by the even-handed way that the author dealt with both aspects of the country to which he was passionately devoted.

I thought, perhaps naively, that this very readable account of Israel's development might have the effect of broadening Lenny's perspective and modifying some of his more dogmatic views.

When I collected Lenny's things from the hotel room, I tossed that book, along with several others that I found on a shelf, into a large canvas bag that I carried home and stored, unopened, along with Lenny's other possessions. Now, when I emptied the bag, I noticed for the first time that an inch or two of white paper was protruding beneath the book's lower margins. Curious, I opened the book and withdrew the paper, which turned out to be a sheet of lined notebook paper folded several times and placed inside the front cover. It contained a handwritten letter addressed to me. I unfolded it, sat back in my chair, dusted off the arms, and read as follows:

My Dearest Brother William,

Knowing how you feel about my returning books you so kindly lend me, I am counting on your diligence in this regard to retrieve this volume and to check its condition upon its return, as is your habit. And when you do so, I assume that you will find this letter, my final one to you, placed between its covers. I have placed it there because it is intended for your eyes only. I know that you will understand my thinking and my reasons for the action I am about to take. Others may not—I am thinking here of Alice—but I leave it to your judgment as to whether or not you share these inarticulate reflections on my life with her and/or your children.

First, about the book you so generously lent me. I found it stim-ulating and engaging, although for my money the author seemed a bit too taken with his own importance. I believe, however, that entertaining as it is, this book is seriously flawed. I know that you hoped that it would have a beneficial effect on me, showing me, by means of an overview of Israel's history, how narrow and limited my point of view is.

Perhaps, in fact, my perspective is just that, but it will take a more seasoned and objective historian to get this hidebound brother of yours to move off his ideological duff. In my opinion, the author of this book does not write history as it was, but as he wished it had been. He tells the story of our people from the perspective of a naïve, willfully blind liberalism. Disregarding the truth, he allows himself the freedom to alter facts to prove that the only way forward for Israel is to pursue a secular, Godless path; either that, or to embrace that watered down and vacuous version of our religion called Reform Judaism.

So although I am afraid that your mission has not met with the success that you hoped for—I am aware that having to contend with such a hard-assed brother has been a life-long trial for you—I am grateful for your thoughtfulness in wanting me to become acquainted with this challenging book. Also, for so much more; above all for your generosity in sharing yourself and your wonderful family with me all these years. You have been all that I could have asked for in a brother. You have been a dear friend.

Obviously, I am alive and able to write this letter and to convey these admittedly sentimental final thoughts to you. However, were it not for you, I would no longer be in a position to write this, as I would not be breathing.

As you may have deduced by now, your friend, Ahmed, came here to kill me. His reasons for this were first of all, enmity. He has reacted with fury to my defense of and unflagging support for Israel, a country that he despises. This I understand. However, there is another reason, and for this I do not hold myself responsible. Or, if I am at fault at all, I can only be charged with the misdemeanor of unrestrained enthusiasm.

Aside from my love for, and support of, Israel, what Ahmed and his coterie of Muslim extremists have objected to is my willingness to grant the request of my mentee, a twelve-year-old boy named Marco, to learn about Judaism. Accordingly, I undertook to share with him what knowledge of our people's history and customs I have managed to accumulate over the years. Objective observers, I believe, would judge my account to be fair, if rendered sympathetically to the Jewish nation.

Ahmed and his group, however, have disagreed. They have charged me with spreading anti-Arab propaganda. This, I must say, infuriated me as I made every attempt to present a balanced view, assigning praise and blame to Jew and Arab alike according to the facts of the case.

Outraged by this unjustified attack, which I can assure you was fueled by the Muslims' long-standing antipathy to Israel and to Jews in general, I struck back. If there is one important lesson we Jews have learned, it is the importance of standing up for ourselves.

Well I did a bit of sleuthing and uncovered information about Ahmed and his lackeys that had them over a barrel; not only that Ahmed had joined some kind of radical group when he was out of the country, but that these self-righteous Muslims were out and out thieves. Ahmed's cronies, Mohammed and Abdul, had their sticky fingers in the honey pot, pilfering money from the Center's funds and using it to bankroll some kind of phony school. Talk about propaganda. That's their stock and trade.

Anyway, I made the mistake of leaving evidence that I had against them, a bunch of phony invoices, on my desk when I left the room one day and this goon, Abdul, found them.

You can guess what that meant. I had the power to blow these *gonifs* out of the water, so they needed to get rid of me fast, *tout de suite* as we say in French. The job was delegated to Ahmed, who arrived at my door an hour ago with that purpose clearly in mind.

How can it be, then, that I am still alive and writing to you, you may ask? And the answer is, you, my dear brother. You have been my shield and my armor. What do I mean, you wonder? Well the short answer is your and Ahmed's relationship whose strength, given the long absence it has endured, may surprise you, as it did him. But there it is, a bond, no doubt fed, as you would say, by unconscious and unknowable forces. In any case, what happened was this: Ahmed arrived here with a plan, quite an elaborate one I may add. His idea was to make my death look like suicide, which he began to do by holding a gun to my head and tying a lamp cord around my neck.

In the end, though, he couldn't go through with it. He started to tighten the noose several times, but each time he stopped. Finally, I asked him what was going on and he blurted out your name. He kept thinking of you, he said, and the friendship you two have had and how much pain doing me in would cause you. I was flattered by this and I like to think it is true. But, frankly, I think he was thinking of the pain he felt when he lost his father. Whatever the reason, he couldn't finish the job.

As I've thought about what, by any measure, is highly unusual behavior, certainly not what you'd expect from someone pledged to carry out Jihad, I've decided that Dr. Ahmed is one of those people who do not really know themselves from the inside out, who don't know their own kishkes. My friend, Birnbaum, is like that. Years ago, he signed up with this mad man, Meir Kahane, who was out to kill as many Arabs as possible. Kahane recruited Birnbaum, who went to Israel and was assigned to blow up an Arab market. He followed orders and went to the market, but could not set off his bomb. Every time he tried, he was unable to go through with it and finally he realized that blowing up people is not for him. He thought it was, but he forgot who he is. Birnbaum is a vegetarian. Killing animals and people are the same for him. He cannot do it and it looks to me that Ahmed is the same way.

He joined a radical group that obviously endorses violence, but Ahmed found out, like Birnbaum, that he can't pull the trigger. He's been a doctor too long. When it comes down to it, it goes too hard against the grain to take a life, even if it belongs to someone like me, whom he very much wants to see deceased.

And the fact that I am your brother and that he imagined your face when they raise the sheet at the morgue and you recognize this all too familiar puss under there was the final deal breaker. It seems that even though we are related, he remains very fond of you.

Anyway, he finally gave up the project as not his thing and he informed me that if I am interested in living, I need to get out of there. Once the others find out that he's botched the job, he said, they will be coming to finish it. He figured I have, at most, a couple of hours before they show up. This gave me an idea. Let me digress here for a moment, William, and explain something to you.

I have been living a lie for more than four decades. I am a gay man who cannot be gay, or, more precisely, who has to degrade himself to carry out acts that I do not even enjoy. In that respect, I am an all-around loser. I cannot live a normal life—as you probably know, I have envied you that for years—and I cannot even live a deviant one. If I allow myself to engage in homoerotic behavior, I feel not only dirty but dishonest. I have concealed who I am from the people I love most and have acted against my own religion, my deepest beliefs.

I have been tortured, William, and I am very tired. Living this way has exhausted me. You were kind enough to help me do something meaningful in my life. Working at the Center with that wonderful boy, Marco, has meant a great deal to me. For the first time in my life I have felt that I was doing something truly useful, something of value for another human being. But that is gone now. Mrs. Green does not want me anymore. I know that. She has been told by people she listens to that I am destructive, a harmful influence on children; that I spread anti-Arab propaganda and am turning an innocent boy against the Muslim people. No matter what anyone says, you or anyone else, she no longer trusts me and will not allow me to work with Marco, or any other child for that matter. I am finished at the Center and I don't have the energy—or the will—to look for anything else.

I am tired, William, and I need to rest now, to go home to our parents and to find peace with them. Do not feel sad. It is what I want and what I need.

But I am not going without a plan. Mohammed and Abdul, those devout soldiers of Allah, are coming to kill me. No doubt they will adhere to Ahmed's plan and attempt to make my death look like a suicide. I am prepared for that, prepared to cooperate, to let them succeed, although they will think that I am being coerced and am yielding only at gun point. They do not know that I have written this letter to you, that you know who my killers are, and that you will take the necessary steps to make sure that they never have the chance to kill again.

This will be my small contribution to Society, and if I do say so myself, a novel way to kill two birds with one stone: suicide by murder; a unique way to do what I wish and catch a couple of *gonifs* at the same time.

I know that you understand what I am doing. You have always been in my corner and have wanted only the best for me. Please be assured that I have thought long and hard about this plan and I am secure in my conviction that it is the right course. You have been a bright light in my life, but my existence has not been an easy one. I look forward to some rest.

Your loving brother,

Leonard.

After I finished the letter, I laid it next to me and just sat there. I don't know how long I remained that way, perhaps half an hour, maybe longer. Then I picked up the letter and read it again, slowly, trying to take it all in, to be in my brother's head, to feel what he felt. But I was too confused, too numb to do that very well. Instead I went downstairs, walked into the den, and closed the door. I wanted to be alone, to let whatever was inside me come out. It took some time, but at last it came, the grief, the pain, the guilt. So much guilt. I felt I had let my brother down in the worst way. I hadn't seen the truth because I hadn't wanted to see it, hadn't wanted the burden of knowing. And so I did nothing to help him, nothing to ease his pain, to help him live with who he was, and perhaps find a partner to share his life. I had been willfully blind and now it was too late. All I had now was the solace of knowing that his death was not in vain, that it would do some good. That is, if I could do my part. As a source of comfort, it was precious little. But it was all I had.

I wanted to tell Alice, to share the letter with her, to talk about it, let out my feelings, and grieve with her. But I recalled what Lenny wrote, and I understood his concern. Alice would be quick to judge. She couldn't help it. Her mind was practical, tuned into the real world. She faced problems and sought solutions. She had no patience for self-indulgence that, in her mind, was concealed behind the idea of self-reflection, of looking inward. For her suicide is, ultimately, a selfish act, an extreme form of indulgence that totally disregards its effect on others, the ones left behind. She did not buy the idea that people who commit suicide are in terrible pain and that they do not have the capacity to think of others, that they can think only of finding relief. Alice did not believe this. She thought it a rationalization for an act of cruel self-involvement and I knew that she would think that way about Lenny. She would point out that he had many options, that he could have come to us or obtained professional help, but that it was his stubbornness and his adherence to a ritualistic and empty Orthodoxy that prevented him from taking positive steps, ones that would have spared us, as well as himself.

I did not want to hear any of this and have to defend my brother against her. Nor did I want to contend with that part of me that agreed with her and that was furious at my hard-assed brother.

So I just sat in my den, sat with the grief and the pain and the anger. Then, when I could speak, I called Barney. He needed to know, but I also felt that he would understand. There was something tender about Barney, something knowing. We talked until I was talked out, until everything poured out of me—including the shameful feeling that in some part of me I felt relief, that a burden had been lifted from me—that I was no longer responsible for my brother.

"I know what you mean, Doc," Barney said. "That's the way it always is when a family member is needy and alone. We take care of them, do what's needed, and push away any thought that they are a burden. And when they are no longer here, we feel guilty for feeling relief. It was that way with my mother. I loved her, was devoted to her, and when she got sick and needed me to be with her, I was there. It was my job. I wanted her to live to a hundred, but when she was gone, I realized I could breathe again. And I felt guilty as hell for that, for liking to breathe."

I thanked Barney for those words, for trying to reach out to me in the way he did. Then we were quiet. Just the two of us and a few moments of silence.

Then Barney spoke.

"Murder by suicide. Brilliant. Who would have thought of that. Turned the *gonifs'* scheme on its head. Outsmarted them and brought them down. Lowered them with their own petard, you could say."

I smiled. "My brother had a good *kup* on him, Barney."

"Absolutely. The man was an original, and what he did will save a lot of lives."

Barney then fell silent. He looked pensive, sad. When he spoke again, he seemed to be thinking out loud.

"We haven't seen the end of this story," he said. "At least I don't think so. Very likely we'll see a replay, only this time the suicide and murder won't be linked. The murder will come later."

I didn't know what Barney was talking about.

"Think for a minute, Doc," he said. "Think about what Ahmed did. That was suicidal, and he knew it."

Now I got it. Barney was saying that there'd already been a second suicidal act. And that the second murder would follow.

"That looks like the scenario," he said, "unless your friend knows how to spin an awfully good yarn. His buddies are going to hold a magnifying glass to every word he utters. If they get a hint of the truth, he's a goner.

"And there's nothing we can do?"

"At the moment, pray and sprinkle a little magic dust, if you happen to have any. If, somehow, we find out what his boys are up to, we'll flash him a warning."

I knew that Barney was right and a wave of fear took hold of me. And with it, a flash-image of Ahmed on the floor of his apartment, a belt around his neck.

Then I shut my thoughts down. After Barney's letter, I couldn't bear thinking of more death and murder. I told Barney I needed to rest and I started to get to my feet.

He held up a hand, "Just a minute, Doc," he said, "there's one more thing. But before I say anything, I need your promise that you won't immediately call Bellevue. It may seem that way, but I'm not actually madder than usual."

With that kind of introduction, I could not imagine what kind of lunacy was coming next. Barney plunged right into it.

"Let me ask you a question," he said. "Are you sure your brother wrote that letter?"

I was sorry I made the promise. The man definitely belonged in Bellevue. Before I could say anything, though, he pressed on.

"I ask for a reason," he continued, "so please bear with me. When I was on the force, we were blind-sided by a situation just like this, fooled by what looked like a bona fine suicide note. It was a perfect imitation of the dead guy's handwriting. In fact, he was murdered by an angry employee who happened to be an ace forger and who turned out fifty-dollar bills in his spare time. I don't really doubt your brother wrote the letter," he added, "but I wouldn't want to under-estimate Ahmed. They don't come any sharper than Dr. A.

"It's not beyond possibility that he could have gotten hold of something Lenny wrote and mimicked his style and way of thinking. Or he could have forced your brother at gunpoint to compose that letter. Not likely, I grant you, but at this point we don't want to be suckered again. Better to check out a remote possibility than to have more egg on our faces. I know a handwriting expert I can consult, a lady who used to work for the NYPD. She is probably ninety-five by now, but totally with it. She's detected hundreds of forgeries. Even the best in the business couldn't get anything by her. If it's okay with you, let me have the letter and a sample of Lenny's handwriting. I'll be back with an answer tonight."

To me this was pure Barney, this need to pursue a way-out idea that he had hooked onto and that now had a hold on him. When that happened, there was no dislodging it. He had to run with it and I had to run along. So I placed the letter and one of Lenny's birthday cards to Emily in a manila envelope and set it aside for Barney to pick up. It was a typical card, complete with Lenny's trademark expression, 'Wishing you a year of good health and good luck,' and signed in his unmistakable hand, 'from your affectionate Uncle Leonard.'

I was sitting alone in the den thinking of all that had happened, of how in a matter of minutes, my world had turned upside down when my cellphone rang. It was Laura.

"I'm in shock, Bill," she said. "I need your help. You were absolutely right. I thought you had a chip on your shoulder, that for some reason you had it in for Ahmed and the others. But what you told me is absolutely true. I sat the three of them down and made them talk, told them I would have nothing to do with any of them if they didn't. So they opened up. You should have heard Mohammed carry on. I had no idea of the rage in him. The man has hatred in his soul. I never saw this side of him. Israel and anything or anyone connected with it is the enemy to be destroyed. He is out for vengeance and I don't think he will stop at anything. Listening to him I was chilled to the bone. And, frankly terrified."

"And Ahmed?"

"He, too, was terribly upsetting, but different. I know Ahmed's story, know what he's been through, and my heart has always been with him. I've loved him and still do. Probably always will. But until tonight, I've not known the full truth. He's told me of his need to become active, to get off the sidelines and join the fight, but he never told me exactly who it is he's teamed up with. He knew what my reaction would be. These are Jehadists pledged to eradicate all enemies of Allah, all non-believers, including totally innocent people.

I fully understand what motivates Ahmed, how his people's suffering has touched him, and why he's concluded that only violence, only blow for blow, can bring about change. But this is murder, and I cannot endorse murder or be with someone who does. Ahmed knows this, so he tried to shade the truth. But it's in the open now and we are going to have to deal with the fallout."

There was anger in Laura's voice, but the pain came through, the pain and the deep hurt. She tried to go on, to say more, but tears flooded her and she had to break off.

I called into the phone that I was coming right over, and within minutes I was out the door. I had put Laura into this situation and I needed to go to her, to comfort her, to try to ease her pain.

And I was frightened for her. My fear that the Arabs might turn against her if they perceived her as a danger to them now seemed a reality. They had opened up to her, not only because she threatened to exclude them from her life if they didn't, but because they trusted her as someone who was on their side and could be of help to them.

Now if they viewed her differently, as hostile to their philosophy and mission and in a position to hurt them, they might very well act against her. I was thinking here of Mohammed and Abdul and their vicious attack on me. I had no doubt that if the Arabs felt sufficiently threatened, they would make a move. And there was no telling what that might entail.

I was also afraid that Laura might come upon the recording device. If she did, the hurt she would feel at discovering that I'd planted it despite knowing how strongly she felt about the use of this tactic, would be a fresh wound, one that, coming on top of the pain she had just endured, would be unnecessary cruelty.

That I would be responsible for inflicting such an injury on someone I had come to care deeply for added to the need I felt to get to Laura's side, to keep her safe, and to prevent her from discovering what she was bound to experience as a callous deception.

I was at her place in fifteen minutes.

Chapter 17

As soon as she opened the door I could see that Laura was drained. Her face was still tear-stained. We greeted each other with light cheek kisses, and once inside, I headed for the living-room. I wanted to make sure that the pen recorder was where I left it. Laura accompanied me, and as we chatted, I maneuvered to a spot inches from where I had hidden the pen.

With Laura standing a couple of feet away and facing me, however, there was no way that I could make a move. When there was a pause in the conversation, I suddenly turned my head to my side, imitated a spastic cough, and feigning discomfort, asked if I might have a glass of water.

When Laura was safely out of the room, I reached behind the lamp to the place where I had concealed the pen—and felt nothing. With rising panic, I swept a hand all across that area. Nothing there. I dropped to my knees and quickly searched the floor beneath the table. I could see no pen, no object of any kind. Hearing Laura coming back, I jumped to my feet and tried to conceal the fright that was taking hold of me. When Laura handed me the glass of water, I took a long swallow and in as casual a voice as I could manage, asked about the missing pen.

"By the way," I said, "I think I may have left a pen here. I was standing near this table, scribbling a note to myself, and I think I put the pen down and just forgot to take it when I left. Did you happen to see a rather large black pen, kind of thick around the middle?"

"I didn't," Laura replied, "but I haven't cleaned the room as yet. I'll keep an eye out for it."

"And you didn't notice anyone else pick something up from the floor, did you?" I was afraid the pen might have rolled off the table and was spotted by one of the visitors.

"I just wondered. That pen happens to be a favorite of mine. I hate to lose it."

"I didn't and no one mentioned finding anything. I'm sorry. I know what that feels like. If I didn't make a point of reminding myself to hang on to my wits, I'd lose half my possessions. But I'll keep looking. It is liable to turn up someplace."

"Thanks."

I knew then that we were in big trouble. One of the Muslims had gotten hold of the pen; either picked it up from the floor or noticed it behind the lamp and took it from its hiding place. Whatever happened, it was clear that they were in possession of the device, and , as Barney had warned me, no doubt they knew what it was. And they would think that Laura had betrayed them, that she had rewarded their openness with traitorous deception.

Given that belief and the fact that Laura now had damning information about them, she had become a very real threat. If she went to the authorities with what she knew—and her traitorously recording their conversation suggested that she intended to do that—very likely they would be arrested for conspiring to commit acts of terrorism.

No question now that Laura was in real danger, and at that thought, a panicky feeling took hold of me. My reaction must have shown on my face. Laura noticed right away that something was wrong. She reached out and touched my arm.

"Bill, are you okay? You don't look well. You're very pale. Are you sick?"

"I'm okay. I just had a spasm in my throat. Nothing serious. I'll be fine in a minute."

"Are you sure? Do you want to lie down for a bit?"

"No, really. I'm okay. But what I really need is a stiff drink."

"I have some good brandy in the house. Would you like some of that?"

"Actually, what I'd like to do is to go out for a drink. I need some fresh air. It would do you good, too."

I didn't want to alarm Laura, but I needed to get her out of the house as quickly as possible. I pictured the Arab's rage at what they believed to be her betrayal and imagined that, seeking revenge, Mohammad and Abdul had armed themselves and were on their way back here. In fact, I imagined the two of them outside the house even now, watching and waiting for the right moment to strike.

If that were true, they would have both of us in their sights, two of the people who had evidence against them—Barney was the other—and were in a position to do them harm. I didn't know if in thinking that way I was being perceptive and reading the situation correctly, or if I was simply reacting out of fear. Barney's words, however, reverberated in my ears; his urging me to follow my nose, heed my inclinations, and listen to whatever feelings arose from within, no matter how bizarre they seemed. And these signals were telling me that it was imperative that we get out now, get to a public place where the presence of other people would afford a degree of protection. Although I was aware that my fear was magnified by the prior attempt on my life, I was certain of one thing; the Muslims were not going to sit around waiting for the FBI to come calling. They would be coming after us; me, Barney, and now, very likely, Laura, as well. We needed not only to watch each other's backs, but to have the equivalent of eyes in the backs of our heads. If I hadn't sensed danger on that dark road, looked back and spotted what was coming at me from behind, the cops or the Sanitation Department, or whoever was sent to do the job, would still be out there picking up the pieces of what was left of me.

Laura had no idea what was happening, but I said I would explain later and hustled her out of the house. We took a cab to an Irish pub in the area, one I liked for its warm ambience, sat in a booth in the rear, and drank scotch. And I explained.

Laura was not at all happy with what I had done, but now having heard for herself the intensity of her Arab friends' feelings, their passionate hatred of, and wish to destroy Israel and its people, she was a bit more tolerant of my use of the recording device. She still regarded it, though, as an underhanded and illegitimate police tactic.

We sat in the Pub for a couple of hours. At that point, I figured the coast was probably clear. If the Arabs had returned to Laura's place and found no one there, they were unlikely to come back so soon.

I got the bill, left cash on the table, and we started for the door. We were seated at the rear of the pub so it was a fair distance to the front door. We made our way slowly, walking side by side, our arms almost touching. Outside it had turned dark and the temperature had fallen.

Despite the weather, Laura wanted to walk, but I convinced her that it would be far more comfortable to jump into a cab. Besides, I wanted to get home before Barney arrived. He had called to say that I had been right about the letter. His expert had confirmed that Lenny had written it and there was no evidence that it had been written under duress. We arranged to meet at my place as soon as we both could get there. We needed to plan our next move.

At that point, my idea was to drop Laura off and head home, but when we reached her house, she asked me to come in for a while. She still felt quite shaken by what she had learned the previous day and she did not want to be alone.

I was glad to oblige. I rang Barney, told him I'd be delayed, and while Laura was freshening up, checked out the house and grounds. There was no sign of trouble. Laura then made drinks and we sat together on her couch, fearful but glad to be with one another. Laura put on some music and we listened quietly for some time.

Then I reached out for her and took her hand. She leaned into me and I held her, just held her in my arms. We sat that way, in a caring embrace, for some minutes. We did not speak. The silence conveyed our concern, our love.

Then it was time to leave. I called Barney, told him I was starting for home, and that I would call him enroute to let him know when I expected to arrive.

"How are you getting home?" Laura asked.

"I'll take the bus, the number nineteen stops at my corner."

"I'll walk you to the stop. I need some fresh air."

We started out and Laura took my arm. Our bodies touched as we walked. When we reached the corner, the walk sign was still blinking. We picked up our pace and started across the street, Laura now a step or two ahead of me. To our left, at about fifty yards distance, I caught sight of what looked to be a black van. Then I heard it, the full- throated roar of its engine as it came for us. I jumped back and reached for Laura's arm. All I could get hold of, though, was part of her coat sleeve. I yanked hard. Laura spun toward me, lost balance, and started to fall. I lost my grip and she tumbled backwards, into the road. The right side of the speeding van caught her flank as she fell, propelled her into the air and over the hood. She landed across the road, face down. Her body hit hard, but surprisingly, made almost no noise. Her hair, which had been drawn back and fastened with a barrette, came undone. Strands of it floated in the pool of blood that surrounded her body.

When I lost my grip on Laura's coat, I fell backward and struck my head on the curb. Two yellow-vested GE repairmen were working in the street. They were about ten yards away when the van tore into Laura. Seeing the two of us down, they instinctively split up. One ran toward Laura, the other toward me. I was in pain. My head was throbbing and my vision blurred.

"Are you hurt, sir?" The GE fellow asked.

"I'm okay. Can you help me up?"

He was a big fellow and muscular, and with one arm he reached down and lifted me to my feet. As soon as I was upright, I muttered my thanks and started across the road. Laura was lying near the curb, blood seeping through her clothing. Her legs were slightly bent at the knees and were skewered to one side so that her body seemed bent into an L-shaped curve. A young woman was kneeling next to her, holding an arm, trying to get a pulse. I dropped to my knees and grabbed the other arm. I thought I felt something, a touch of life. Two passersby, a teenage boy in a sweatshirt and jeans, and a short, white-haired woman, were on cell phones, calling 911. Within five minutes an ambulance was on the scene. It came from Lexington, the closest hospital in the area and the one in which Ahmed and I both worked. Before it came to a stop about ten yards from where Laura lay, the rear door swung open and two attendants jumped to the ground. Working quickly, one of the men did a quick inspection of Laura's body and tied a tourniquet around an arm that was bleeding badly while the other slipped a brace behind her neck. Very carefully they lifted her onto a stretcher and slid it into the ambulance. Noticing blood smears on my head, one of the attendants, after getting my story, suggested that I be checked out at the ER. I thought this unnecessary, but I wanted to be with Laura, so I climbed in and sat alongside her.

Just before we started off, one of the attendants, who appeared skilled and knowledgeable despite his baby face, grabbed a stethoscope from a hook and listened for signs of a heartbeat. Hearing something, he reached for oxygen, and quickly affixed a mask to Laura's face.

As we approached the hospital, the driver called ahead and a trauma team was waiting when we arrived. They transferred Laura to a gurney and wheeled her inside where she would be examined and, if still living, x-rayed and prepped for surgery.

A nurse escorted me to an examining room, cleaned my wound, and called the ER resident who looked me over and suggested a couple of stitches to close a sizeable laceration. Out of respect for a fellow physician, he asked if I wanted him to call in a surgeon to handle the job. I did want him to call a surgeon, but not for that purpose. I asked him to page Dr. Ahmed Aslam and to tell him that Dr. Strickman was in the ER and needed to see him immediately.

It turned out that Ahmed was operating, and his page was answered by an OR nurse who promised to deliver the message. Twenty minutes later Ahmed appeared, still in his scrubs, his mask hanging around his neck.

"Siggie, what happened? Are you all right?"

I touched my head. "A cut, nothing serious. It's Laura."

"Laura, my God. What happened. Where is she?"

I gestured toward one of the inner rooms.

"It's bad, Ahmed. She was attacked. Deliberately run down. She's in a bad way."

Ahmed cursed.

"Did you see who was driving, Siggie? Did you get a look at him?"

"It was a van, a long, black van and the windows were blacked out."

Ahmed nodded. "That's what I thought," he said. "Never mind, I know who did this."

He was gone for twenty minutes by my watch. When he returned, he could barely speak. When he tried, he choked. Tear stains blotched his cheek.

"She's gone, Siggie," he finally got out. "They tried everything to bring her back. It was too late. Her heart just gave out."

I said nothing and he sat down next to me. We sat side by side in silence. Finally, I spoke.

"Is she still inside?" He nodded.

"I'd like to see her."

"You should. She was fond of you, Siggie."

I stood up and started toward the rear of the ER. I was nearly out of the room when Ahmed called after me.

"Would you mind if I came with you?"

"Come," I said. "We both should be there."

Laura's body lay on a metal table. It was covered with a sheet. Tubes of various colors were strewn about. An empty IV bottle hung from a stand and a vital signs monitoring machine remained plugged into a wall socket. Its screen remained lit.

I raised the sheet. Laura's face was bruised and swollen, but she still looked beautiful to me. I loved her, had always loved her. I felt as though my heart was breaking into a million pieces. Ahmed stood alongside the table just looking, saying nothing. After a minute or so I started to lower the sheet, but he stopped me.

"Not yet, Siggie," he said. He stood looking for another minute or two. Then he turned to me.

"My father was right, Siggie," he said. "In the end there is only pain. That's what it comes down to. Pain on both sides, only pain. That's what he tried to tell me, but I didn't take it in. I couldn't take it in, Siggie. I thought him weak. In my heart I called him a collaborator who wanted peace at any price, a traitor willing to sell out our people. But he knew,

Siggie, my father knew what happens, what the end is. He knew that after the killing, there is nothing. There is only the pain. He saw it everywhere. He lived with it himself. He told me, but I couldn't hear it. In the end that is the legacy. That's all there is. Pain all around."

As Ahmed was speaking, a number of memories arose from within, memories that took the form of images that appeared briefly, then vanished. I saw the recording pen concealed behind the big lamp in Laura's living room. And I saw myself listening, just listening on the phone, not speaking, not sharing what I now knew about Ahmed. In some part of me I was glad that Laura had turned away from him, that he couldn't have this very special woman. And recalling this scene, I felt deeply ashamed.

Violence comes in many forms, many shapes, I thought to myself. Ahmed's father would have known that. He would have been alert to the concealed kind, the kind not easy to see; not the violence of bombs and guns and speeding cars; the kind, rather, that we carry around with us, that we live with every day, that is part of who we are, of who we have become.

"I wish I had known your father," I said. "I think of him as a very wise man, but I don't know if I could have heard him either. Most likely not. But if I could have, that might have changed things; that could have made a huge difference for me, too."

I reached out and touched Ahmed's arm and we just stood there, the two of us standing together, looking at Laura's body and the metal table and the white sheet. Then we turned and walked out together.

"Meet me at the Center tomorrow morning, Siggie," Ahmed said. "We need to talk."

Chapter 18

After I left Ahmed, I felt an urge to walk, to keep moving and to try to blot out the images that assailed me; the blinking walk sign, the streak of black metal that was the van, Laura being hurled over the hood, Laura lying in a spreading pool of blood. I could not dispel these pictures. They pursued me, followed me everywhere like the furies of old; intrusive, insistent, forcing their way through the barriers I tried to set up and giving me a throbbing headache.

To ward them off, I focused on the pavement, on the street signs and the house numbers, on whatever detail I could find to crowd my brain and bar the door to these intruders. It was a five-mile walk to home and it was not until I was almost at the front door, having waged a largely unsuccessful battle against the relentless furies, that I realized that no defense that I devised, no barrier that I erected, could keep them at bay. They were there because I needed them to be there. It was I who summoned them, I who kept them coming, kept up their relentless assault. They were my punishment and my atonement for what I had done; for being an accomplice to murder.

I stopped twice on the way back, momentary pauses, to call Barney and give him a heads up as to when I expected to be home. On both tries I was unable to reach him—each time the call went to voicemail—so I left a message that I was on my way and expected to at my place in twenty minutes.

When I reached home, I went straight to my den and closed the door. There was no one home at the time, but I had a need to closet myself, to be protected against a danger that seemed immanent, that was waiting to strike me down.

I was not aware of falling asleep in my armchair until I was awakened by the ringing of the phone. A gruff-sounding voice was on the other side of the line.

"Dr. William Strickman, please."

"This is Dr. Strickman."

"Dr. Strickman this is Captain Anthony DiMatto at the 23rd Precinct."

"Yes?"

"I understand that you have been working closely with a former colleague of ours, Barney Siegel."

"That's right."

"Dr. Strickman, I am very sorry to tell you that Barney was attacked by two assailants tonight. He was badly beaten and has suffered a bullet wound."

"Shot? Is he alive?"

"He is alive and in surgery now. That's all we know."

"What are his chances?"

"I can't tell you that Doctor. I don't know. All I can say is that the situation is serious."

"Where is he?" My impulse was to get to wherever Barney was as quickly as possible. I did not want to walk into another hospital and find the body of another person I loved stretched out on a bare metal table.

"Fordham Hospital. It happened in the Bronx. Right on the street. Someone was out to get him."

"I know," I said. "Did he say who attacked him?"

"We don't have that information. When they brought him in, he wasn't in a condition to say much."

"Okay. Thanks for calling. I'm heading over there now."

"All right. Pray for him, Doc. Barney is a good man."

"A damned good man. I'm praying already."

It took me a half hour in heavy traffic to reach the hospital. Barney was already in the recovery room, but no one was allowed in. I sat on a bench in a dim and antiseptic-smelling corridor of the hospital for the next two hours. I was told that a doctor would come by to speak to me, but no doctor showed up. Finally, a nurse appeared and told me that my friend was in the ICU.

"How is he?"

"Holding his own at this point."

"Will he be alright?"

The nurse declined to answer, but led me along the corridor and up a flight of stairs. The ICU was set off from the rest of the floor. There were a dozen cubicles, all occupied, with monitors beeping and buzzing around each bed.

"You can see Mr. Siegel for no more than ten minutes each hour," the nurse said. "And he must not be taxed in any way. He is better, but his condition remains serious."

"I understand," I said.

Very slowly I walked over to Barney's cubicle. He was wired up and heavily bandaged, but conscious. He could speak only slowly, but in a voice that was surprisingly strong. He attempted a smile when he saw me.

"For this you got me out of retirement," he said. "When I signed on, you didn't mention that there are folks out there who don't feature sharing this planet with Barney Siegel."

"The fellow you signed on with was a total greenhorn, Barney," I said. "I had no idea of what we were getting ourselves into. My apologies, partner. I should not have gotten you involved."

"I got myself involved, Doc." Barney said. "I saw a chance to be a big shot, to solve a big-time crime and make the boys at the 23rd sit up and take notice. Not your fault. But if it helps to get rid of these guilt feelings, I will forgive you on one condition."

"What's that?"

"Two pints of frozen yogurt on your next visit."

"You are asking me to bring in contraband material?"

"Call it a peace offering."

"Okay. You've got it. But only if I'm given immunity first in case the docs accuse me of euthanasia."

"It's a deal."

I sat down next to Barney and reached through the railing on his bed to touch his arm.

"How did it happen, Barney?"

"I wish I knew. I was minding my business, walking to the subway to come to your place and the next thing I knew I'd been worked over by a couple of Tony Soprano's boys. I was on the ground and they were kicking the beJesus out of me when a cop car came by and the *Momsas* took off. One of them pulled a gun as he left, got me in the side. A lot of blood, but missed center stage they tell me."

"Thank God. Did you get a look at them?"

"Not really. All I saw were two thugs standing over me. I faked being out cold, but I could feel one of them going through my pockets."

"What were they after?"

"Probably fishing. They must have followed me, saw where I went, and checked out who lives there. Then they figured I might have something on them, so they needed to find out."

"Did they get the letter?"

"Afraid so."

"So now they know what happened in the hotel room."

"And that we know who killed your brother."

"Not healthy for us."

"It's you we have to worry about, Doc. They've knocked me out of the box. You're the one with a target on your back."

"What about Ahmed? Whatever he told them, they know now he refused to do the job. They are not going to be happy about that."

"True, but Ahmed knows the score. I'm concerned about you. You need to take a Fiji Island vacation starting now."

"I'll get right on it, Barney."

"I mean it. You don't have a lot of time."

He was worried and it was not a time for Barney to be agitated. So I didn't tell him about Laura or about the near miss I'd had, that I'd already been targeted. I knew Barney was right, that the best thing I could do would be to get out fast, quit the field, and let the professionals handle the fallout. But I couldn't do that. I was in too deep. Now that the Jihadists were exposed, I felt sure that they would act quickly, that they would feel an urgency to carry out whatever mission they were on. There was no way I could turn my back on this situation. I needed to find out what they were up to. Without Barney, I was on my own. If he were still on the job, no doubt he would come up with some *meshuga* plan that would send us in the totally wrong direction, but I missed the guy.

And I found myself thinking of Ahmed, wondering where he was and what was happening to him. What had he told his cronies about what happened in that hotel room, about not having gone through with his assignment to finish off Lenny? Had he given them a story about suddenly being interrupted by a maid coming in, or a phone call from the front desk, with Lenny tipping them off that there was trouble in his room? Or did Ahmed claim that his gun had jammed and Lenny, tough Lenny, put up more of a fight than he'd expected and he couldn't complete the job alone.

Whatever he told them, they now knew the truth and would be coming after him. I tried to reach Ahmed, to alert him to what had happened, to warn him of the danger.

But I couldn't get through to him. I tried several times throughout the evening, but there was no answer and no message. In fact, it seemed that the line was dead.

That night I had dreams of violence; gun shots, bloody wounds, bodies lying in deserted streets. When I awoke, it was still dark, a menacing kind of 4:00am darkness, and the air was frigid.

I stayed in bed for some time, trying to banish the night, clear my head, and get ready to keep my appointment with Ahmed. Then I rose, and although it was still early, headed for the Center. I hoped against hope that he would be there.

Chapter 19

He was. He was in his office, sitting on a straight-back chair with Abdul standing behind him, seeming to be watching his every move. He was unshaven, his face was drawn, and his clothes were badly rumpled. He looked thoroughly fatigued.

He greeted me with a nod, then motioned for me to come close. As I approached, he reached into a pocket, drew out a torn piece of notebook paper.

"What are you doing?" Abdul demanded.

"I had a dream in the couple of minutes of sleep I got last night. You guys did a job keeping me awake. I hope you enjoyed our extended conversation."

"No time for jokes," Abdul said sourly.

"Well, sitting here's been pretty dull, so I jotted down my dream. Dreams are an interest of mine, a kind of hobby."

"Foolishness. Dream all you want. Dreams will do you no good."

"Actually, dreams can be prophetic, Abdul. We can learn a lot from them. The Qur'an mentions them in several places."

"This means nothing to me. I deal with what is real. That is something you will be dealing with, too, my friend."

"We all need to do that. But you know, Abdul, I think you are missing something. You might find your dreams quite fascinating. Why don't you try writing down one you've had recently? I will help you figure out what it means."

With that Ahmed turned in his chair and held out a pencil to Abdul. At the same time, he reached behind him with his other arm and opened his hand. In it was the piece of paper he had written on, now crumpled into a ball."

I snatched it and slipped it into a trouser pocket.

Abdul slapped at Ahmed's hand, a blow that clearly stung him. He swung back around, clasping that hand, then he turned to me.

"I know I invited you over, Siggie," he said, "but you'll have to excuse me. Right now we are extremely busy. Abdul and Mohammed want me to accompany them to the school building. They are working on an interesting new project and they need my help."

"I understand," I said. "I will be in touch later."

He did not reply to this.

Mohammed had come in and positioned himself alongside Ahmed. Without a word he seized him by the arm and pulled him to his feet. Then, with the two of them, Abdul and Mohammed, flanking Ahmed and seeming to push him forward, the three walked out.

When they were gone, I crossed the room to Ahmed's desk, settled into his chair and withdrew the crumpled paper from my pocket. I unraveled it and spread it out in front of me. At the top of the page Ahmed had written the words, my dream, and in parenthesis, have Siggie decode. Just beneath that he had set down a strange and puzzling narrative. This was the dream.

I am in an old European city. I am standing in front of a building that appears to be about two hundred years old. It is an institution of some kind, perhaps a library or a museum, but it looks as though it might once have been a private home. The entrance is at street level. I approach it and see that the number 19 is displayed on the front door. The door is open and I walk into the entranceway. There, engraved on one wall, are the dates 1891-1938. I proceed into the foyer, which contains an art nouveau table and chairs. On the table is a large book. I sit down at the table and begin to leaf through the pages. The book appears to be some kind of index that contains dates and numbers. On the first page is another date, 1900, which is followed on the second page by the letters, SE, capitalized and written in bold type. On the third page is the number, 4. This is followed on the next page by a third date, 1867.

As I am leafing through this large book, I am suddenly aware that a ghost-like figure has appeared and is standing behind me. I look up. This figure has a menacing look and the appearance of a gangster. On the lapel of his double-breasted jacket is a large nametag on which is printed the letters, S and J. Then, as mysteriously as it appeared, this figure vanishes.

I continue leafing through the book. The next page contains directions to the reader, who is advised to turn to page 1930. I do so and find something incomprehensible. The letters, H.B.U. are printed in large type and beneath them, equally prominent, the number 42.

The following three pages are cryptic. They contain just one word each: glass, smash, and the word, revise. The final page is all black. It looks as though someone has done a thorough job with a black crayon. At the very bottom of this page the word, night, appears prominently, presumably giving a title to the all-black creation. That's all there was. At that point, the dream ended. I woke soon thereafter feeling puzzled and with a sense of impending danger. I quickly write the dream down and try to reflect on it, but I do not get very far. I decide to show the dream to Siggie and feel an urgency to do so.

Here the writing ends. As soon as I finished reading, the associations began. They piled in on me one after the other, flooding my brain so rapidly that I could barely keep pace with them. They were all about dreams, the dream book, and Freud, topics that Ahmed and I talked of often when we were working together. I had been surprised then to discover how much Ahmed knew about Freud's life and his work on dreams. Under his father's tutelage he had studied The Interpretation of Dreams and knew that landmark work as well as many practicing analysts. I told him many times that he had made a big mistake switching from psychology, that he could have done much better than to become a fancy butcher, that he had the makings of a first class shrink, and that we could have been partners. Now, clearly, he was using the knowledge he had of Freud and the dream book to send me a message that only the two of us could understand.

My first associations were to certain details in the dream; the number on the door of the building, number 19, followed by the dates 1891-1938, which were engraved on a wall in the entranceway.

The building and the number 19 were familiar to me, as Ahmed knew they would be. The building reminded me of the Freud Museum in Vienna at 19 Bergasse Street, which I had visited several times. Originally, the museum was Freud's home and office, the place where he lived and worked until the invasion of Austria by the German army forced him to flee the Country.

Clearly Ahmed's dream was focusing my attention on Freud's life in Vienna as the first clue to decoding his message. The date, 1900, and the letters, SE that appeared in the large book on the table in the parlor directed me to the place where I would find additional clues. Nineteen hundred, I knew, was a momentous year in Freud's life. It was the year in which he published what, arguably, is his towering achievement: The Interpretation of Dreams. The letters SE were equally familiar and would be to anyone involved in the field of psychoanalysis. The letters stood for the words, Standard Edition, the comprehensive collection of Freud's works that is our Bible. The number 4 referred to the fourth volume in that collection, the one that contains the Dream Book. What came after that, the date 1867, and the sudden appearance of an unsavory figure, a gangster-type with the letters S and J printed on a nametag, completely stumped me. I tried to associate to these elements in the dream, but nothing came. The associative process which, until then had come to my aid, seemed to have dried up. Eighteen hundred sixty-seven meant nothing to me, nor did the strange apparition that had risen up behind Ahmed in the dream. I needed urgent help from a Freudian scholar or, at the very least, access to a library where I could get hold of a copy of The Interpretation of Dreams. I was pretty sure that these baffling clues referred to that work and that Ahmed assumed that I would understand them. He was giving me a lot more credit than I deserved.

There was only one thing to do. I put on my coat and headed for the exit. Fifteen minutes later, I was in my library at home searching the Dream Book for the date, 1867, and the letters S and J, which appeared in Ahmed's dream.

It was in Freud's report of one of his own dreams that I found what I was looking for. It was in 1867, Freud wrote, that he had a puzzling dream. In it he associated one of his colleagues, S, toward whom he felt envious, with an uncle of his, J, who was a dishonest fellow and who had been sent to prison for a crime that he had committed. Freud explained that in this dream he identified S with J, a criminal, as a way of diminishing S and putting him down.

Now I understood what Ahmed was telling me in this disguised form. The key was the word, uncle. This had to refer to Mohammed, who was not only Abdul's uncle, but who was called uncle by the children at the Center. Ahmed was connecting him with S, Freud's colleague, because Mohammed was Ahmed's colleague, and also with J, Freud's dishonest uncle. He was telling me in no uncertain terms that Mohammed was a criminal. But this was not news. Both Lenny and Barney had discovered

Mohammed's larcenous scheme of preparing false invoices and stealing money from the Center. Ahmed would know that I had been told this and, in addition, that I had a strong suspicion that Mohammed was behind Laura's killing and the attempts on Barney's and my lives. Why then, employ a clue that simply reiterated what I already knew? Ahmed, I figured, was getting at something else, most likely that Mohammed was going to commit another crime and that had to do with the big downtown event that Ahmed had mentioned to me. Ahmed was alerting me to what was going to happen; he was sending me a warning.

What this was all about, though, what kind of attack—if that is what it was—was going to take place. I had no idea. Thus far I had discovered nothing that gave me a hint, nothing in the Dream Book that clarified what Ahmed was getting at.

I focused again on the dream and on the pages in the large book that held the last of the clues. There was the page that displayed the letters B.H.U and the number 42, followed by the pages on which was printed the words, glass, smash, and revise. And there was the page that was colored black with the word, night, featured in large type at the bottom.

I had no idea what any of this could mean. These clues, such as they were, seemed impenetrable. I scanned the Dream Book for a connection with any of them and found none. Ahmed was now using some other frame of reference, but what this was, I couldn't begin to guess.

For assistance I turned to my old standby, to the only source of help I had in a situation like this. I sat myself down in my favorite chair, an overstuffed bear of a thing, leaned back, and let my mind wander.

What it wandered to was a surprise. I pictured the outside of my house, followed by what seemed like a visual tour of the downstairs. First I saw the foyer, then the living room where I was seated. This was followed by a view of our dining room, and, finally, the kitchen.

The camera then panned over the room before focusing down on the kitchen table where Alice was sitting. She was eating breakfast and doing what I had seen her do hundreds of times before; attempting to solve a puzzle in the morning paper. This was not the usual crossword, but a puzzle made up of scrambled letters that had to be re-arranged to make comprehensible words. Alice often tackled such puzzles, and to my amazement—I am a hopeless dud at such things—was often able to solve them.

This old scene, I figured, was an association to the puzzle I was contending with; Ahmed's mysterious clues. My unconscious was telling me something, but what?

For some time I drew a blank. Then, all at once, it struck me that the scene of Alice working a particular kind of puzzle, one involving scrambled letters, was itself the message; Ahmed's puzzle, I figured, was just that kind: a matter of letters that had to be unscrambled. To make any sense of it, I had to approach it that way.

I looked at the letters B.H.U. and began to play with them, to juggle them. First I tried the arrangement, U.B.H, but this sparked nothing by way of connection, nor did H.B.U. Initially the alternative, HUB stimulated little more, but it was a word and that was a start. I printed the letters H.U.B. on a slip of paper and let my mind associate to the word, hub. The first thing that came to mind was that a hub is the center of something, the core from which other elements radiate. We speak, I thought, of the hub of the city, referring to its center, or the hub of a rail system, its central point, the place from which tracks radiate out in all directions.

I recalled then that in the large book of letters, B.H.U. was followed by the number 42, so I added that to the rearranged letters. This gave me H.U.B. 42, and a light went on somewhere in my head. To a New Yorker, H.U.B.42 signified one thing, and one thing only; Grand Central

Station, the hub of the metropolitan railway system, located at 42nd Street and Lexington Avenue.

I turned next to the words, glass and smash, which appeared on the following two pages. These were followed by the word, revise. Following that came the all black page with the word, night, printed on the bottom. I had found these clues by following the directions to turn to page 1930. That number, too, I thought, must have significance. What, I wondered, connected these words and the page number. And what was the relevance of a black page and the reference to night? There was only one obvious connection: the color, black, and the word, night, were clearly related. The blackness symbolized and emphasized the essence of night, the absence of light being the cover for the dark deeds that take place at that time. As for the other words, glass and smash, my associations took me far afield. What came to mind was a wedding ceremony, a traditional Jewish one. As part of such a ceremony, the groom breaks—or smashes—a wine glass under his heel. This symbolizes the end of the bride's virginity, a break with the past, and the beginning of married life. This connection struck me, however, as one of those unhelpful associations that leads one not closer to an answer, but farther away; that points in the wrong direction. It was highly unlikely that the Arab, Ahmed, would know anything about Jewish weddings, and it was even less likely that such a reference would appear in his dream. It was true, though, that Ahmed knew quite a bit about Jewish history. His father, who had corresponded for years with Israeli psychiatrists and had studied for a year in Haifa, had insisted that Ahmed acquaint himself with the Old Testament as well as the history and customs of their closest neighbor. 'One day,' his father had said to Ahmed, 'there will be peace between our peoples and you will want to understand who they are and what they believe in.'

I was always impressed by Ahmed's knowledge of Jewish holidays. In fact, when we worked together, it was often he who reminded me that one was coming up. We also discussed the Holocaust a good deal, and although Ahmed assigned some blame to the Jews for alienating others by their insular and xenophobia attitudes, thus bringing hostility upon themselves, he had a deep appreciation of the devastation of the Holocaust and condemned the Nazis for their genocidal tactics. It was not the Jewish people, per se, he often said, who aroused his fury, it was the die-hard Zionists, those zealots who stole his people's homeland and drove them into the dessert.

It struck me then, that maybe my initial association to a Jewish ceremony was not entirely off track, that I had intuited that there was a reference to something Jewish in these last few clues, to an experience involving the Jewish people.

I searched my mind for another possible connection between something Jewish and the breaking of glass. And it came to me from nowhere, first appeared in my mind as a series of images; Nazi youths smashing the windows of Jewish businesses and Synagogues, burning books, looting the homes of Jews and beating their inhabitants; images of the infamous night in Berlin known as Krystallnacht. It was this night that marked the beginning of Hitler's campaign to exterminate the Jews. Ahmed and I had often talked about that night and argued about the cause of the blind fury that fueled it.

That must be it, I thought. Ahmed was making reference to the night of the broken glass, and telling me, warning me, that another such onslaught, another Krystallnacht was about to take place. This must be the downtown event, I thought, the big event that required such careful planning. It was going to happen now, tonight. That was Ahmed's message.

But what was the target? Where was this onslaught going to take place, and exactly when? I looked back at the sequence of clues, looking for one that might contain the answers. What immediately struck me was that there was only one clue that referred to a place; H.U.B.42, or

Grand Central Station. No doubt this was a prime target for a terrorist attack. The station was always busy and a well-placed bomb there would wreak havoc. There would be untold casualties.

But something did not fit. If Grand Central was the target, why the reference to Krystallnacht and the attack on the Jews? That had to be important. It was clear that Ahmed was saying that the attack would be on a Jewish Site. It would be another Krystallnacht. I was sure that somewhere Ahmed had provided information as to the location of the attack. Somehow I had overlooked it. Or had I seen it and not recognized its importance? Worse yet, had I recognized the clue and simply not been able to decipher it?

I felt discouraged, discouraged and frightened. If I failed at decoding the message Ahmed had sent me, I would be responsible for a true catastrophe. I thought of Barney lying in the hospital. I had dragged him into this mess and caused him needless suffering. And unless I could solve the puzzle that I was holding in my hands, his suffering would have been in vain.

I returned to the dream. There had to be more significance to the reference to Grand Central Station than I understood. Also, to the word, revise, and the number 1930, the page to which I had been directed.

I tried associating to the name, Grand Central, and the words, grand, and central, separately. All I could come up with was something that seemed not at all connected with either of them or with Grand Central Station, the name of the neighborhood temple which I attended, Bet Sholom, and immediately thereafter, a photo-like image of the face of the young man, Myron Klein, who was our cantor. I could not imagine what possible relevance this image had to the matter of urgent concern: the location of the attack planned for tonight. I had learned, though, not to dismiss any association that came to mind, no matter how irrelevant, or even bizarre, it seemed. There was usually some kind of connection with what preoccupied me at the moment. So I stayed with what my unconscious had thrown up and tried to recall whatever I could about the cantor. I searched my mind and came up only with the thought that Myron had a remarkable tenor voice. But then something came back to me, something I knew but had totally forgotten. Myron would soon be gone; he would no longer be our cantor. Two months previously he had announced—to general consternation on the part of the membership—that he had accepted an offer to become the chief cantor at a larger and much grander synagogue. This, in fact, was the one at which Lenny had been Bar Mitzvahed and where he had remained a member for over four decades. This was the famous Central Synagogue, a landmark building in New York and one of the most beautiful houses of worship in the City. Ahmed's dream contained clues to that name that now, in retrospect, seemed obvious but when I first encountered them seemed impenetrable. Both clues, the name Grand Central and the word revise, referred to Central Synagogue. The name, Central, and the locations of each, centrally situated in the City, were common to both. Moreover, both can be said to be Central to, and at the hub of, their respective systems, an East Coast rail system, and the reform movement in Judaism. If I missed this connection, Ahmed threw in the word, revise to help me along. To revise is to redo, remake, or—this was the clue—reform. Central Synagogue is a leading Reform Synagogue in New York and one of the most distinguished in the world. Ahmed was taking no chances with his old student.

I knew now the target of the planned attack. And the association with Krystallnacht told me that it would take place at night and would be no minor operation. Another Krystallnacht meant bombing and fires and major destruction. What I did not know was when the assault would take place. To prevent it, we needed that information and it had to be somewhere in the dream.

There was, however, no mention of time, nor any reference to it. Or was there? I had assumed that the direction to turn to page 1930 was an indirect reference to the year 1930 and was somehow linked to the attack on the Jews in Germany.

But what if the number 1930 did not refer to a year, but to something else; to a designation of time. Nineteen thirty might not refer to the year 1930, as I had assumed, but to 1930 hours. In other words, to 7:30p.m. Greenwich time.

Once that thought occurred to me, I knew it was right; the attack, Krystallnacht, would be launched at Central Synagogue at 7:30p.m. tonight. I had managed to decode Ahmed's dream, and for a brief moment I felt a surge of pride, and with it, an image of myself showing off to Ahmed—bragging about what I had accomplished—and proving what a skilled dream interpreter I had become.

Then I came back to the moment. It was now close to noon. If we were to thwart this attack, we needed to get moving; to plan and launch a pre-emptive strike was a complex undertaking. It would take time. Clearly I needed to inform the authorities immediately. But then it hit me. What was I to do, call the police and tell them that I had uncovered a terrorist plot by interpreting an Arab's dream? No doubt that information would be met with the response reserved for kooks and psychotics. A polite thank you followed by private laughter and rapid dismissal of my report. I needed Barney, needed him desperately to run interference for me, to speak to his buddies and vouch for me; to get them to listen and to respond. But I could no longer lean on Barney. I was on my own. I could hear his voice, though, urging me to act, telling me that I had earned my badge as a bona fide member of the gumshoe squad and that his buddies at the 23rd would hear me out; that they would be respectful of Barney's pal. With that voice in my ear and my heart rising into my throat, I made the call.

Chapter 20

I was right—and wrong. When I called the 23rd, I reached a Detective Richmond and introduced myself. At first, he was interested in what I was saying—any report of a possible terrorist attack puts the police on alert—but as soon as I mentioned a dream he relegated me to his crank file.

"A dream? Are you telling me you got this information from a dream?'

"Not an ordinary dream, Detective. One that contained a secret message that I had to decipher."

"And who was it who sent you this message?"

"One of their group. His name is Ahmed, he's a doctor, a surgeon. We worked together at one time."

"I see. In other words, this Dr. Ahmed is an undercover agent. He is one of us, is that what you are saying?"

"No, he's one of them. One of their operatives."

Let me get this straight. You are telling me that this Dr. Ahmed is one of the bad guys and that this bad guy tipped you off about an attack his group was planning? Why would he do that?"

"You'll have to ask him, Detective. My guess is that he woke up from a bad dream."

"I see. This terrorist wakes up from a bad dream and proceeds to have another dream that he writes down and gives to you because you are a shrink and shrinks like dreams.. And this second dream gives away the store. It puts the *kabash* on their operation and is bound to get him and his buddies arrested. Do I have that right?"

"That's about it, Detective."

"No offense, Doctor, but this makes zero sense. Nothing adds up. Let me ask you something. Have you been having any memory problems recently? What you're telling me sounds like your own dream."

I could make no headway with the man. I used Barney's name but he wasn't impressed.

"If you can bring Barney down here, maybe he can explain all this to me. None of it computes."

He clearly wanted to get rid of this nutty friend of Barney Siegel's.

"I'll tell you what I'll do, Doctor," he said, by way of dismissal. "I'll speak to my Chief, fill him in on what you've told me. If he thinks your info warrants it, he'll put in a call to the FBI. We have a direct line to their New York office. In any case, someone will probably get back to you. The FBI gets a lot of kooky calls, but they are pretty good at following up on them."

"Look, Detective, there is nothing kooky about what I'm telling you. This is urgent. Unless we act now to stop these people, there is going to be a slaughter in this town tonight. A lot of innocent people are going to lose their lives. In fact—and I am not exaggerating—this is going to be the biggest assault on this City since 9-11. You've got to contact the FBI immediately."

Detective Richmond's idea of handling this kind of thing was to repeat what he had just said. He was immoveable. The best I could do was to get the name of their FBI contact out of him. I hung up and made a second call.

I had more luck this time when I used the phrase, imminent attack. I was put through to the Director's office. His name was Ray Adelson and it turned out that he knew Barney. They had worked together on a case some years before. Barney had contacted him after we made our after-hours visit to Mohammed's school and found out what kind of place it was.

"We put them on our watch list right after that," Chief Adelson said, "and we have been monitoring their activities since. We expected them to make a move, but not this soon."

"Their hands were forced. They knew we are on to them."

I did not go into their efforts to eliminate us. That long story would be for another time.

"And when is this attack supposed to take place?"

"Seven-thirty tonight, according to our information. They are targeting Central Synagogue, no doubt figuring the sanctuary will be packed for the evening service."

I did not mention the dream.

"That information is solid?"

"Absolutely. They are using their school in the factory building as a front for their operations."

"How do you know that?"

I filled Adelson in on what I knew about the phony school and how Mohammed and company were using it to indoctrinate young people from the Center with their anti-Israel, anti-American propaganda.

"I can't say more," I added with a sense of urgency. "A man's life is at stake."

Adelson nodded. He'd been in situations like this before.

"The building that you mention, is that where these people are now?"

"That's my understanding. They are doing their final planning there and will be leaving early this evening to launch the attack."

Chief Adelson nodded. "Okay. We'll mount an operation to intercept them. By the way," he put in, "I heard about Barney. How's he doing?"

"I haven't heard the latest. He was mauled by a couple of thugs and had a bullet wound in his side when they brought him in. He was bleeding badly."

"Doesn't sound too good. Will you be checking on him today?"

"I was planning on doing that soon. We can call him together, if you like. He'll be glad to hear from you."

"Okay. We can call in a couple of minutes. First I need to give the order to get our operation underway. We have a plan for this kind of raid. We'll infiltrate the area around their school building with anti-terrorist police and specially-trained FBI agents. We'll also have marksmen on nearby rooftops. They'll be no way these people can escape. I'll give them five minutes to surrender. After that we'll smoke them out."

"You are talking about tear gas?"

"That usually does the job. Drives them into the open, but if they hole up and try to shoot it out, there'll be no survivors. They'll have no chance against our fire power."

"Let's hope they realize that. We want one of them alive, a fellow named Ahmed. He's given us valuable information."

Chief Adelson shrugged.

"All depends on what they do," he said.

At that point Adelson suggested that we try to reach Barney.

"He gave us the first tip about this cell. I'd like to keep him informed as to what we are planning. He knows these people. He may be able to give us some useful input, that is, if he is well enough to talk."

"Barney Siegel could be in a comatose state and he would still find a way to put in his two cents," I said. "He'd wake up long enough to do that."

Barney had been moved to a private room. I got the direct line and dialed. A nurse picked up."

Barney Siegel is being examined right now," she said. "If you can hold on for a few minutes, the doctor will talk with you."

After a short wait, Barney's surgeon, a Doctor Finley, came on the line. I'd met him when visiting Barney, and now he talked to me doctor to doctor.

"Your friend developed a wound abscess," he said, "and we had to go in and drain it. We cleaned it out and added another antibiotic."

"And how has he responded?"

"Surprisingly well. He's a tough nut, this partner of yours. Now that he is on the mend, he's already campaigning to be let out of here. Says he's getting withdrawal symptoms from not getting his fix of frozen yogurt."

I found myself smiling. It was the kind of involuntary smile that comes with a sense of relief.

"That's Barney. He can withstand a bullet in the gut, but without his pint of strawberry at bedtime, the man is an invalid. Let me speak to him."

"I'll put him on, but he's still a sick man. Please don't get him agitated."

"Not to worry. I'm his personal tranquilizer."

"You are stonewalling me," Barney said when he came on, "You are colluding with these doctors to keep me out of the loop."

"Nonsense. I've been collecting good wishes from your pals on the detective squad. They've voted five to three to wish you a speedy recovery."

"Tell them thanks. With a vote of confidence like that, I may come out of retirement."

Then Barney's voice turned serious. "What's been happening, Doc? I worry when I don't hear from you."

"Everything's under control," I replied. "We are about to close down our Muslim friends and their school."

I then told Barney everything, caught him up on Ahmed's dream, the message it conveyed, and the plan Ray Adelson had to stage a raid on the school building.

"Where is he now?"

"Who?"

"Ahmed."

"He's still with the others."

"He hasn't managed to separate from them?"

"I don't think he can. When I saw the three of them at the Center, Mohammed and Abdul were keeping a close eye on him. They had him surrounded. It's pretty clear they were guarding him."

"I'm not surprised. Don't forget when they hit me, they got hold of Lenny's letter. They know why Ahmed didn't finish the job. Of course they know about his friendship with you. But this is different. This makes him a turncoat, a collaborator with the enemy. They are not going to let him out of their sight."

I knew that this was true, but somehow, having been caught up with the dream and the challenge of decoding it, Ahmed's situation did not register on me. It took Barney to lay out the truth.

Chief Adelson took the phone, and after extending good wishes to his old comrade, outlined the operation he had planned. After he had finished, Barney asked to speak to me again.

"They are going to kill Ahmed," he said. "You know that, don't you?"

"What do you mean?"

"There is no way Mohammed and Abdul are walking out of there waving a white flag. They are out to kill cops and to die doing it. And they will. So will everyone up there. No one will survive once Adelson's crew opens fire."

Barney's words coursed through me like high voltage current from a downed power line that I had stepped on without ever seeing it. There could be no doubt about it. Ahmed had doomed himself. He was almost certain to be killed. Barring a true miracle—and I had long ceased to believe that miracles existed outside the minds of people addicted to wishful thinking—Ahmed would be riddled by police bullets, bullets from the guns of the very people who, through me, he had reached out to in the hope of preventing the slaughter of scores of Jews. I imagined Ahmed, before he decided to act, before he decided to write out and hand me his dream, struggling with himself, struggling over whether or not to take that step. I thought of him pondering over the fact that among the Jews he would save would be many who had little sympathy for him and his family, many who despised Arabs and thought of them as dirty people, as criminals who wantonly killed their Israeli neighbors.

He detested such attitudes and, in his heart, blamed that kind of thinking for the suffering of his people and their inevitable retaliations against their persecutors; efforts to strike back that the Israelis, with their willful blindness, saw only as criminal acts, as acts of hatred and unprovoked aggression. But then I imagined Ahmed thinking of his own father and appreciating, as he had not done before, that were the attack to take place, people would die who had as little to do with the Occupation and the actions of the Israeli army as his father had with the murderous acts of Hamas; that these people were as innocent of wrong doing as was Laura, who wanted only to understand the beliefs and values of those who were influencing her child; whose only wish was to raise him in an atmosphere of tolerance and understanding. And I imagined Ahmed recalling what his father had tried to impress upon him; that Jews prayed to the same God, no matter by what name they called him, as he himself did, as Muslims everywhere did.

I had a sudden image of Ahmed being struck down, of bullets ripping into his body, of his collapsing, dying. I felt a searing pain in my gut. I grabbed the phone and shouted into it, "We can't let that happen Barney,"

I yelled. "They can't kill Ahmed. Don't let them. Tell them, Barney, tell them we need him, that he is one of us.

For a few moments there was no response. There was only silence. I didn't know if Barney was still there or whether, with nothing more to say, with no solution to offer, he had simply put down the receiver. Finally, his voice came through.

"Put Adelson back on," he said.

I handed the phone to the Chief, who had heard what I'd said and took the receiver reluctantly. He put it to his ear and listened for under a minute. Then he responded.

"We'll do what we can, Barney," he said. "But you know what these situations are like. If a firefight breaks out, there will be no controlling it. It will be a free for all. The lives of our men will be on the line. They need to be free to react spontaneously. The delay of even a second can mean the difference between staying alive and taking a bullet in the head. I can't order our people to hold their fire. They need to protect themselves. And that means shooting at anything that moves up there. You know what I'm saying. You've been there yourself. Our job is to eliminate the threat to us and anyone else in the vicinity. And first and foremost, I need to protect my men. If we can do that and also spare your guy, we'll do that. But it's not likely to happen that way. You understand what I'm saying, Barney. The odds are against anyone walking."

Adelson hung up and turned to me.

"Barney wants me to take you up on the roof so you can identify this Ahmed, point him out so I can alert our men that we want him alive. First of all, it's against regulations to involve a civilian that way, to put you in that kind of danger. And even if I were to disregard the rules and do what Barney wants, it's not likely to work. The only chance this fellow, Ahmed, has is if he separates himself from the others, goes into another room, or at least removes himself from the line of fire. If he's in the same place with the other two, the same room, or at the same window, there's nothing we can do. We'll have to take out everyone up there. We can't take a chance. Even one of them left standing is a menace to us. One gunman could devastate us. We can't take that risk."

"I understand," I said, "but the two main guys up there are not going to let Ahmed separate. They are going to watch his every move, make sure he stays close."

At that, the Chief simply shrugged, "Nothing we can do then," he said. "Let's hope that doesn't happen."

Then he reached out and touched my arm.

"This Ahmed is someone you care a lot about, isn't he?" he said.

I nodded

"Well I won't ask how it happened that a friend of yours got mixed up with a gang like these terrorists who kill innocent people and claim they are doing the Lord's work," he said. "That I don't understand. But I guess that is your business. If I were in your shoes, though," he added, "I'd pray to the real God, not their phony one. A genuine God would never condone such barbaric behavior. He would never allow innocent people to be slaughtered. I'd pray to that one, the one with a heart, to hide your friend, put him in a closet, get him away from these murderers."

"That's just what I plan to do," I replied.

"And if we can, if there's any way of doing it, we'll lend him a hand," Adelson said.

Chapter 21

"If I let you come with us, I'll need you to follow orders, do exactly as I say," Adelson said to me after we rung off with Barney. "We don't want anything to happen to you. You need to stay with me at all times and keep yourself out of harm's way. I'm doing this strictly as a favor to Barney. I owe him. But if anything happens to you, he'll never forgive me."

"Nor will I. But not to worry. My specialty in the Army was keeping out of harm's way. I'll be fine."

It was almost 2:00p.m. then, the time that Adelson had set to gather his team together and issue final instructions for carrying out the operation that he dubbed SL One, short for Statue of Liberty, number one. Adelson had hit on that name, not as a salute to the actual Statue of Liberty in New York Harbor, but in remembrance of the trick football play called the Statue of Liberty that his high school football team had used to win the State Championship.

The chief motioned to me to follow him into a conference room in which his team had assembled. There were fifteen squad members, composed of a mix of plainclothes police, FBI agents, and specially trained sharpshooters. At the front of the room, which was buzzing with noisy and nervous chatter, was a lean tower of a man, six foot five and rugged looking, with a substantial nose and fashionable stubble on his face. He wore a grey business suit with no visible indication that he was high up in the police hierarchy. In fact, this lanky giant, whose name was Timothy Parnes, was the Deputy Commissioner in charge of anti-terrorist operations. Chief Adelson introduced us and explained that I would be joining his team as a spotter. He did not say more than that and Timothy Parnes did not ask. He simply extended a very large hand and offered a hearty, "Welcome aboard, Sir."

Adelson then went to a blackboard and outlined the plan that he had worked out to carry out the raid on the terrorists' headquarters. As he did so, he drew a series of X's and O's on the board in the manner of a football coach.

"At the termination of this meeting, we will proceed to our staging area, which is a parking lot two blocks north of the entrance to this building," Chief Adelson said. "Four unmarked cars and a van will be waiting for us there. A team of five squad members will occupy each of three vehicles. Our four marksmen and their equipment will be transported in the van. Commissioner Parnes and I will follow in the fourth car, along with our spotter for this operation. Adelson did not mention me by name, perhaps not wanting to arouse curiosity as to why an outsider had been added to the team. In any event, Adelson's omission met with neither question nor comment from the group.

"We will proceed to the neighborhood of the target building," Chief Adelson continued, "and park our vehicles well out of sight of its occupants. The team will then proceed on foot in groups of two or three to slip into their designated places surrounding the building. Our target is an old factory building, no longer in use for that purpose. On the fourth floor of this building the men we are seeking operate a school that purports to offer religious instruction. We have discovered, however, that this so-called religious school is a front for the operation of a radical Islamic cell that spreads anti-American, anti-Israel propaganda. It is here that these terrorists purport to teach youngsters from the Youth Center about religion, but actually fill their heads with this kind of propaganda.

We believe that the ultimate goal of these people is to recruit some of these kids to join radical groups.

"The school is also used as the group's headquarters. They store their weapons there and use it to plan their operations. We have information that they are doing that right now, planning an attack on a mid-town synagogue, one of the oldest religious sites in the city. Such an attack would wreak havoc on our city and result in an untold number of casualties, including many deaths. Our job is to stop this operation before it starts and to break up this cell."

Chief Adelson then went on to spell out the details of his plan. The team would surround the building and cover all possible exits as well as any escape routes that the Muslims might try to take. The marksmen would be on the roofs of adjacent buildings with their weapons trained on the groups' fourth floor headquarters. He, himself, along with the Commissioner and their spotter, would also be on a nearby roof. He would direct the operation from there.

"If at all possible," Adelson added, "we would like to take these men alive. They have information about other cells operating in the US that would be valuable to us. We would especially like to capture one of them, a man named Ahmed, whom we believe is ready to cooperate with us. Our spotter is acquainted with this man and will identify him for us. If it is possible to take him alive, we should make every effort to do that."

Adelson then filled in some details about the procedures to be followed.

"When our team is in place," he said, "I will use a bullhorn to let the Terrorists know that they are surrounded by armed law enforcement officers and that they have no chance of escape. And I will order them to come out with their hands in the air. If they do not respond, we will use teargas to flush them out. But if they fire on us, we will return fire immediately and without restrictions. In that event, your orders are to shoot to kill. Remember that we are here to prevent these people from launching an attack on our city."

Adelson then gave the signal to move out, and the cars started for the target area in Harlem at one minute intervals. I was in the last car with the Chief and the Commissioner. We proceeded slowly and in silence, the three of us looking out our windows to make sure that we had not been spotted as plainclothes police by the denizens of Harlem with their uncanny instinct for sniffing out the law.

The operation came off as planned. The police vehicles were parked on a side street two blocks away from the school building, and proceeding slowly in groups of two or three, our team slipped into position. In short order the target was surrounded and all escape routes covered. The sharpshooters took their places on two adjacent rooftops, and at a few yards distance from one of the marksmen, Adelson set up his command post. The Commissioner stood on one side of him and I placed myself a few yards away on the other. On the way over, the Chief had distributed binoculars to us, and as soon as I took my place on the roof, I trained them on the fourth-floor windows. The three large windows of the main classroom faced us, as did a fourth smaller office window, separated from the others by three feet of a brick wall. I focused first on the two windows, then on the single one. I was searching for Ahmed, but saw nothing but empty rooms. There seemed to be no one there.

Adelson was in radio contact with a Captain on the ground, and when he got word that all was ready, he picked up the bullhorn at his side and made his announcement. His voice echoed in the valley between the buildings like the voice of a wrathful God issuing a doomsday warning.

There was no response. We waited the full five minutes that Adelson had given the Terrorists to surrender without a sign either of movement or sound coming from the fourth floor.

Adelson held the radio to his mouth and was about to give the order to employ teargas when the sound of a single shot broke the silence and a policeman crouched behind a parked car fell backwards. The shot came from the farthest corner of the classroom windows. Instantly an explosion of return fire tore through those windows and caromed off the surrounding brick. The firing from our side kept up for several minutes. There was no response from the fourth floor, and no one was visible in the classroom. I scoured the room for Ahmed, but saw no sign of him, no sign of anyone. Adelson waited, bullhorn in hand, for any sign of life on the fourth floor. He waited to see if anyone had survived the withering assault from below. I imagined all of them, including Ahmed, riddled with bullets, lifeless on the classroom floor.

After several more minutes of silence, Adelson picked up the bullhorn and issued another warning to whoever might be alive. There was no hope of escape, he reiterated, so that if anyone wished to stay alive, he needed to appear at the front door unarmed and with his arms in the air. There was no response of any kind. Only silence. Adelson then ordered the use of teargas. Before a single canister could be launched, however, the barrel of an AK47 poked through the small office window and rapid bursts of fire caused the men below to take cover. I caught sight of Abdul's face at the window, and for a brief moment, I thought I saw Ahmed standing behind him.

Abdul fired, ducked out of sight, and fired again. He repeated this sequence four times, and on his last effort managed to score a hit on a cop who darted out from behind a parked car and was struck in the chest as he broke into the open.

The return fire was intense, and when Abdul next appeared at the window, he was unable to get off a shot. No sooner did he rest his weapon on the windowsill than he himself disappeared. I was watching the window and I saw him approach, begin to place his gun on the sill, then suddenly vanish. He did not reappear and I imagined him wounded and dying on the floor.

A minute later, I spotted Ahmed. He was carrying a rifle and was moving slowly toward the vacated window. There seemed to be someone behind him, pushing him forward. A few seconds later he appeared at the window. Again I thought I saw someone behind him. Suddenly he turned, as though to face that person, then stumbled forward and had to hold onto the window frame to prevent himself from falling. I was sure that he had been pushed.

When I saw what was happening, I called out to Adelson.

"That's him, that's Ahmed," I shouted. "That's the man we want. They are holding him prisoner, pushing him up front, making him a target. Tell your men to hold fire."

I was sure that Adelson heard me, but he acted as though he heard nothing. He did not respond in any way, and it was clear that he had no intention of doing so. He was going to let Ahmed be killed. In fact, as soon as Ahmed appeared at the window, he was met by a barrage of gunfire. Instantly he disappeared from view and did not return to the window. I imagined that, as with Abdul, his luck had run out, a bullet had found him, and he lay dead or dying on the classroom floor.

A few minutes passed in which no fire came from the fourth floor, and, again, I could see no one moving around up there. Then, just as I thought the fight was over, I spotted someone approaching the window. Then the muzzle of an AK47 appeared, and, behind it, I spotted Mohammed's face. He leaned out and fired two rapid bursts which tore into the trio of parked cars that shielded a half dozen policemen before he dropped out of sight.

Seeing this through his binoculars, Adelson again gave the order to employ teargas and within minutes we could see clouds of gas rising from the doorway and behind several windows that had been shattered by the canisters. For six minutes by my watch stillness again descended on the building. No face appeared at the fourth-floor windows and there was no further gunfire. Then what looked like a whitish-grey towel appeared at the small window. It was spread across the entire window. After a half a minute or so, the window was raised and an arm reached out and started waving the towel. Adelson radioed the Captain below to hold fire. Then he picked up the bullhorn and directed it at the terrorists. He acknowledged their signal of surrender and ordered them out of the building.

In less than a minute they were at the entrance, the three of them forming a line. Ahmed appeared first at the threshold. He held his arms high, palms outward. Moving very slowly, he walked toward the police line. Directly behind him and partially hidden by him, Abdul and Mohammed stood close together. From a distance they seemed tethered to one another. They were carrying assault rifles, and as they emerged from the shadow of the entranceway, both made exaggerated thrusting gestures toward the ground, as though wanting to make sure our side saw that they were ridding themselves of their weapons. Then, with a simultaneous maneuver, like synchronized dancers, they dropped to their knees, spun in opposite directions, and opened fire. Abdul brought down two policemen, including the Captain, who was standing some thirty yards in front of him. Mohammad also hit his target. Bullets from his gun ripped into Ahmed's neck and back. Their force drove him forward and he took three quick steps, as though starting to run, before he collapsed.

I was on the move instantly. I made a dash for the small roof door and tore down the five flights of stairs to the ground. Twice I lost balance and both times came close to going down hard on my face.

When I reached Ahmed, two cops were squatting beside him. One was feeling for a pulse, the other trying with his hand to stem the heavy bleeding that was coming from a large cervical wound. A third cop standing nearby was on his cell phone calling for an ambulance.

As I approached, running, I blurted out that I was a doctor. The police immediately made a space for me and I dropped to my knees and leaned over Ahmed. He was conscious but breathing irregularly. When he saw me, Ahmed murmured something and made a motion for me to move closer. He could barely speak, but he managed a few words.

"You did it, Siggie," he said. "You finally got a dream right." He paused, took a deep breath, and added, "You are definitely coming along."

I wanted to respond, to say something, to tell Ahmed what was in my heart, to tell him that he was the best teacher I'd ever had, that we were still a team, but I couldn't speak. I couldn't get anything out. All I could do was to press a handkerchief to Ahmed's wound and grasp his hand, grasp it and hold it tight.

He tried to smile, but couldn't quite make his muscles obey. I leaned in closer and touched his face. His breathing had become erratic. There were longer intervals between breaths. He tried to speak again, but couldn't. Instead, he managed to raise his right hand and point to the breast pocket of his shirt. He seemed to be indicating that there was something in there that he wanted me to see. I reached in and extracted a small snapshot. It was a picture of Ahmed's father standing in front of what looked like the facade of an auditorium of some kind. On the front of the building there was a sign that bore the letters, IPA, and next to it some words in Hebrew that I could not make out. IPA, I knew, was the abbreviation for the International Psychoanalytic Association. The picture must have been taken, I thought, when Ahmed's father was at a meeting of the IPA, perhaps the year it was held in Israel. I held the photo up and looked closely at Ahmed's dad, the person I had heard so much about over the years. He appeared very much as I imagined him; a strong and vigorous-looking man. But what struck me most forcefully was how much the two of them, Ahmed and his father, looked alike. They had the same solid frame, the same determined expression on their faces, the same mop of black hair that had a way of falling over one eye, and the same mischievous smile.

Ahmed looked up at me, raised his right hand, and pointed again. First at the photo I was holding, then directly at me. Then he settled back. A moment later he took a deep breath, a long breath that was followed by a last heaving movement of his chest. Then he was still.

I remained on my knees and looked at Ahmed's face, just looked at it for several minutes.

"I get it, Ahmed," I said to him, "I understand. I'll hold onto him. I'll keep him with me wherever I am."

The photo was still in my hand. I held it up again and took another look. There was no doubt about it, no one could miss the resemblance. These two were father and son. Ahmed had wanted me to see that, to take it in and know that it was true.

I reached inside my jacket and slipped the picture into the breast pocket of my shirt. It was in the same place in my shirt as it had been in Ahmed's, in the place closest to his heart.

I stayed on my knees for another minute or so and found myself doing something I hadn't done since I uttered the words at my father's funeral some two decades earlier. I recited the few lines of the Kaddish, the Jewish prayer for the dead, which I could remember. I knew that Ahmed would understand.

The policeman standing behind me had his hat off and was standing tall, as though at attention, but when he saw me starting to rise, he reached down and offered me a hand. I had just gotten to my feet when my phone rang. It was Barney on the line. Before he could say anything, I shouted at him, lost control, and just screamed into the phone that Ahmed was dead, that Mohammed had murdered him.

Barney was silent. For a moment he said nothing, but I could feel his presence, feel his reaching out to me.

"You've lost another brother," he said. "When it came down to it, he had your back. And you were right, Doc," he added, "You called it. The man was a *mensch*."

I nodded as though Barney could see me. Then, trying to hold on, I changed the subject.

"Where are you?" I asked. "What's going on?"

"I'm home," Barney replied. "I went AWOL

"What do you mean?"

"Signed out. They weren't doing a thing for me."

"What are you talking about?"

"Just poking me around the clock and hooking me up to all kinds of tubes when I wasn't looking. And when they were not doing that, they were shoving bed pans under my ass, refusing me the privilege of taking a leak on my own recognizance."

"Maybe the doctors wanted you at bed rest."

"What they wanted was to show the world that they are the greatest, that they can perform miracles like keeping relics like me alive."

"I heard that you are the one who surprised them, that you were making an amazing recovery."

"The fact that I am still breathing after these doctors got through with me qualifies as a major surprise. What amazes me is that I survived their starvation regime. They refused me even a cup of my yogurt. I went on strike, wouldn't eat a morsel of the gruel they serve in that place. Finally they gave in, or seemed to. Actually, they tried to pull a fast one, the old bait and switch game. They got me primed for a fresh cup of Chobani, then when I am all hot to go, the dietician switches to Junket. Claims they ran out of the good stuff but that Junket is the in thing, that it is the new Chobani. That's when I signed out. When I was a kid my mother tried to pull the same stunt, telling me Junket beats out chocolate pudding any day. I didn't fall for it then and I wasn't about to now. I've had enough of this kind of double dealing."

"I get it. But are you going to be okay?"

"I'll be fine. A couple of weeks of my old lady's brisket will put me back in the game. I'll be on the job before you know it. But what's been doing?"

I told Barney about the police raid and described how Ahmed had been gunned down.

"I got him killed, Barney," I said. "I tipped off the police. If it wasn't for me, that wouldn't have happened."

"No, Doc, it wasn't you who did that," Barney replied, "It was Ahmed. He handed you the dream knowing exactly what would happen, that he was unlikely to survive. He knew that. He wanted to return to himself, to who he really was, and he needed you to help him do that."

"Maybe so."

"There is no question, Doc. He knew that you'd understand, that you'd get his message, and that you'd do what he needed you to do."

I said nothing. My thoughts went from Ahmed to Laura and back again, to the love they had for one another and the love I had for them; love all knotted up with the other part, the jealousy, the wish to harm, to ruin their possibilities, their chance to experience a kind of joy in each other that I deeply envied. And I thought of Barney and how I'd dragged him into this crazy business and where he'd ended up.

"You know, Barney," I said, "If I hadn't started this whole thing, Laura would be with us, she'd be with Marco and Ahmed, and you'd be sneaking out your back door for your nightly fix instead of lying in bed trying to patch up a hole in your gut."

Barney's reply was quick. He did not hesitate.

"You loved Laura and she loved you back. You tried to protect her and you did what you could. But we can't always do that. Sometimes the evil out there wins out and we lose the people we love. Nothing harder, but it's pain we have to live with. And as for me, you got it wrong, Doc. Before you came along, I was fading away, sinking into my grave before my time on a steady diet of empty days and TV nights. I was already looking like one of those prunes I take for constipation. No, I'm glad you made that call, Doc, that you remembered Barney Siegal."

"You are not the kind of person one forgets, Barney."

"It's reciprocal, Doc. By the way, what's our next job? Has anyone been looking to do in another member of your family?"

"Not yet."

"When they do, keep me in mind, I need the work."

"I'll do that, Barney," I said. "The next time I'm about to start a murder investigation, I'll call. A partner like you doesn't come along every day."

For a moment Barney didn't speak. Then his voice came through, a bit husky.

"Actually, I could say the same about you."

"We turned out to be a team, didn't we? He added, "You earned your badge. You know how to use that *kup* of yours."

"Up to a point, Barney. But then I run into myself, into the part of me that pulls the shades down, that wants to live in the shadows."

"I know what you mean, Doc. I've seen you hide out that way. I've felt like shaking you, telling you to wake up and turn on the light. Talk about self-deception, about the way people fool themselves, I've wanted to tell you to look in the mirror. That's State exhibit number one. Next time, though, it won't happen— I'll be watching. Anytime you start with the excuses, start telling yourself stories, I'll be on your tail. To me that's what a good partner needs to do; stop his pal from putting on blinders. You were on the couch a long time, right, Doc?"

"Seven years."

"And you are still into hiding from yourself. Give me three weeks, a month, and I'll have you dealing yourself a straight hand, playing with your cards face up. How does that sound, Doctor?"

"Tough and scary. I don't know if I'm ready to sign on with a hard ass like you, but I guess I can give it a try."

"Okay then. It's a deal. Next time there's trouble and you can use another *altacocker* on the case, give me a ring. I'll be down there on the double. And remember, you never have to worry. There's no statute of limitations on a promise from Barney Siegal. That's one item that never runs out."

Acknowledgements

As always, I want to thank my wife, Mickey, for her continued encouragement and belief in my writing and for her endless patience with the many long hours I spent working on this book.

Thanks to Albert Zuckerman who kindly read and did editing on an earlier version of the manuscript and for his valuable suggestions.

My deepest gratitude to Marie Annicelli who, with grace, good humor and amazing skill, was able to decipher my illegible handwriting, and with much forbearance, put up with the endless changes that I made in the manuscript. Without her unflagging help over the past fifty years, I could not have published any work at all.